"You're just trying to distract me,"
Margo teasingly complained.

"Why not?" Bruce asked. "Turnaround is fair play and you certainly distract me. Lean forward," he said, his eyes on hers.

She did as requested but asked, "Why?"

Ever so lightly he traced the outline of her lips with his index finger and succeeded in getting them both excited. He'd forgotten what it felt like, to feel this way around a woman.

His pulse accelerating to double time, he touched his mouth to hers. All it took was a touch, and he felt himself intoxicated. There was no doubt about it, she made his head spin. Not a good way to go if he had work to do.

Bruce drew his head back, fighting off the temptation to kiss her again. "You do make everything taste better."

Dear Reader,

Happy Valentine's Day! What better way to celebrate than with a Silhouette Romance novel? We're sweeter than chocolate—and less damaging to the hips! This month is filled with special treats just for you. LOVING THE BOSS, our six-book series about office romances that lead to happily ever after, continues with *The Night Before Baby* by Karen Rose Smith. In this sparkling story, an unforgettable one-night stand—during the company Christmas party!—leads to an unexpected pregnancy and a must-read marriage of convenience.

Teresa Southwick crafts an emotional BUNDLES OF JOY title, in which the forbidden man of her dreams becomes a pregnant woman's stand-in groom. Don't miss *A Vow, a Ring, a Baby Swing.* When a devil-may-care bachelor discovers he's a daddy, he offers the prim heroine a chance to hold a *Baby in Her Arms,* as Judy Christenberry's LUCKY CHARM SISTERS trilogy resumes.

Award-winning author Marie Ferrarella proves it's *Never Too Late for Love* as the bride's mother and the groom's widower father discover their children's wedding was just the beginning in this charming continuation of LIKE MOTHER, LIKE DAUGHTER. Beloved author Arlene James lends a traditional touch to Silhouette Romance's ongoing HE'S MY HERO promotion with *Mr. Right Next Door.* And FAMILY MATTERS spotlights new talent Elyssa Henry with her heartwarming debut, *A Family for the Sheriff.*

Treat yourself to each and every offering this month. And in future months, look for more of the stories you love…and the authors you cherish.

Enjoy!

Mary-Theresa Hussey

Mary-Theresa Hussey
Senior Editor, Silhouette Romance

Please address questions and book requests to:
Silhouette Reader Service
U.S.: 3010 Walden Ave., P.O. Box 1325, Buffalo, NY 14269
Canadian: P.O. Box 609, Fort Erie, Ont. L2A 5X3

Marie Ferrarella

NEVER TOO LATE FOR LOVE

Silhouette
ROMANCE™
Published by Silhouette Books
America's Publisher of Contemporary Romance

To Mama,
for teaching me,
by example,
to never give up.

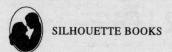 SILHOUETTE BOOKS

ISBN 0-373-19351-3

NEVER TOO LATE FOR LOVE

Copyright © 1999 by Marie Rydzynski-Ferrarella

This edition published by arrangement with Harlequin Books S.A.

Printed in U.S.A.

MARIE FERRARELLA

lives in Southern California. She describes herself as the tired mother of two overenergetic children and the contented wife of one wonderful man. The RITA Award-winning author is thrilled to be following her dream of writing full-time.

Dear Reader,

I was very close to my mother, both when I was growing up and when I became an adult. There were times when she was the best friend I had in the world. I'm happy to say that the tradition continues. My daughter, Jessi, and I are very close, and this is something I really treasure. Despite some of the more vocal talk shows, I really believe that more mothers and daughters are close than not. Which is why I loved doing the two books that comprise LIKE MOTHER, LIKE DAUGHTER.

We've already done Melanie's story, now it's her mother Margo's turn. A fiercely independent and extremely energetic woman, Margo has forged a path for herself and her daughter, believing that the one perfect love everyone dreams about only exists in the movies her aunt Elaine loved so well. And her new son-in-law's dad, Bruce, believes he's had his shot at the one perfect love and it's now over. But it's never over, is it? And it's never too late to fall in love with that one special person who makes you feel as if you're walking a couple of inches off the ground. This is what happens to Margo and Bruce despite themselves. They find love they never expected. If you haven't yet, I hope you will, too.

Love,

Marie Ferrarella

Chapter One

Like a hot summer wind rolling across the desert in August, Margo McCloud burst through the doors of St. Michael's Church in Bedford. The sound of the cab pulling away from the entrance faded into the background as she struggled to juggle a suitcase in one hand, a garment bag with her newly purchased gown in the other.

"Damn traffic," she muttered under her breath, swallowing the more vehement sentiments occurring to her in deference to where she was. She hated arriving anywhere late, even if it wasn't her fault. A big rig, suffering a blowout, had overturned on the freeway, transforming a forty-mile trip from the LA airport into a three-hour ordeal. On top of that, she was still suffering from jet lag. Her point of departure had been Athens, Greece.

This definitely wasn't her finest moment, or her steadiest, especially when she collided with the six-foot-four-inch frame of a man who'd chosen that exact moment to stand on the other side of the door. The resulting impact would have sent her sprawling to the floor if, at the last moment, two very large, very capable arms hadn't closed around Margo, catching her.

Focusing, Margo drew back some of the air that had just been knocked out of her.

The stranger raised his dark brown brows in amused surprise and smiled.

"Margo?"

It didn't really surprise Margo that the man who had just collided with her knew her name, even though she didn't have a clue who he was. She'd met a world of people in her time. She was bound to forget a few now and then.

Though, she amended as she straightened, slowly leaving the protective hold of the man's arms, it wasn't likely that she would have forgotten him very easily. The man was nothing short of gorgeous, in a warrior-hunter sort of way. If warrior-hunters were given to wearing tuxedos.

Where had he ever found one to accommodate such broad shoulders?

"Yes, I'm Margo." And then a sliver of concern slipped through. Had she gotten her time confused on top of everything else? Distress crept into her voice. "I didn't miss it, did I?"

Bruce Reed was immediately struck by the energy that swirled around the woman. Must run in the family. Looks certainly did. He could easily see the resemblance to her daughter. It was there, around the eyes and the mouth. And, of course, there was the hair color. Both women had hair the color of wheat in the bright morning sun. Melanie wore hers long, while this woman's hair was done up, showing off a very delicate neck that contrasted quite nicely with her very strong chin.

The sign of a fighter, Bruce thought.

Mother and daughter, eh? He wondered if this was what his son was going to be up against in another fifteen years or so. At least the view was nice.

"No, you didn't miss it," he assured her.

With a nod of his head, Bruce indicated the double wooden doors leading to the inside of the church. The last time he'd looked, it was crammed full of people, including his very nervous son, all of whom were waiting on Margo's arrival.

"Melanie insisted that they delay the wedding. She refuses to get married without you. I'm the lookout." Aptly named, he decided, because the line, "Look out, here she comes," occurred to him as soon as he set eyes on Melanie's mother.

His eyes slid down the slender, athletic frame. There, too, the women resembled each other. Small-boned, well proportioned. He couldn't help wondering if he was being out of step with the times, noticing that. Probably. He'd lost track of what was acceptable behavior and terminology between men and women these past fourteen years.

"This way, please." He took her arm, relieving her of her suitcase. "Melanie's quite a girl, um, I mean woman," he corrected himself.

"She's both," Margo said, laughing softly. "Most of our species are."

Since he didn't know her, Bruce thought it safer not to comment. Instead, he led her to a side room where Melanie was waiting. Knocking once, he tried the doorknob. It gave easily.

The tiny room required the occupancy of only two people to be crowded, and it already had that. Three almost stretched it beyond the legal limit. To keep from being smothered by a combination of satin, lace and the press of three female bodies, Bruce Reed chose to stand outside the threshold.

He smiled broadly at the young woman he'd known for a very short time and had come to love like the daughter he'd never been blessed with.

"Melanie, I think I have something that belongs to you."

"Mama!" Whirling around from the mirror, Melanie

McCloud exhaled as dramatically as any of the overtrained actresses she'd watched while growing up on various movie soundstages. "I knew you'd make it."

Though it wasn't easy, she managed to throw her arms around her mother. The garment bag fell, landing on the edge of Melanie's gown. Melanie wasn't given to worrying, but as the last few hours had ticked away, she had begun to fear that her mother wouldn't arrive in time for the wedding.

Margo blinked back what felt like a tear. Now? She hadn't cried in years. Years. Now was a ridiculous time to begin. This was supposed to be a happy occasion. Knowing there was little time, Margo still allowed herself a moment to absorb the embrace.

"Of course I made it. It's not every day that my girl gets married." Releasing Melanie, she stepped back to get a good look at her. When had she turned into this beautiful young woman, this little girl who had looked up at her with worshipful eyes? "I'd've come a lot sooner if someone had thought to either stop pumping people into Orange County or build enough roads to accommodate them."

The rest of the diatribe on her lips evaporated as the sun suddenly shone full force through the bit of colored beveled glass that served as a tiny window. The rays of light seemed to form a spotlight, with Melanie as its target.

Margo's breath was stolen away. "Oh, God, let me look at you."

Her mother was finally here. Everything was perfect now, Melanie thought.

Pleased, she tried to hold out the wedding gown's skirt for her mother's perusal. It wasn't easy. Joyce Freeman, her maid of honor, attempted to make her five-seven frame as small as possible as she pressed against the wall to give Melanie more room.

"It's a beautiful dress, isn't it?" The moment she'd seen it, Melanie had known she had to have it, had to wear it as she pledged her heart and her eternal love to Lance. That it fit like a dream was merely a bonus.

"The dress is pretty, *you* are beautiful," the deep voice behind Margo corrected.

She'd almost forgotten about him, Margo thought, looking over her shoulder at her escort. "I think I'm going to like this man." She drew her brows together as she realized that she hadn't asked his name. She was slipping. "Who are you?"

Extending his hand to her, he shook it. Margo's hand was swallowed up in his. For just the tiniest second, she had the overwhelming feeling of well-being. Had to be the occasion, she thought.

"I'm Bruce Reed," he told her. When no immediate recognition surfaced in the flawless face before him, he added, "The groom's father."

"Oh." Figured, the best ones were always taken. Nonetheless, she radiated a smile at him. "Nice to meet you."

When Joyce caught Melanie's eye and tapped her watch, butterflies were instantly back on the runway in takeoff position. "I hate to break this up," Melanie said, drawing her mother around to face her, "but I've got a wedding waiting to start." She glanced at the garment bag that was still on the floor. "Mama, are you going to change into something else, or are you just planning to take that garment bag with you to the pew?"

Margo laughed, brushing her lips against Melanie's cheek. "Always had a smart mouth, didn't you, pet?"

Melanie's eyes crinkled in response. "Matches the rest of me."

Lips pursed thoughtfully, Bruce shook his head. "I'd say it's a little too crowded in here to change. Maybe you'd like to use the rest room?"

Margo waved away his suggestion, narrowly avoiding hitting Joyce. "Don't worry about me. I can manage just fine anywhere."

The limited space presented no challenge to her. There had been a time—a very short time, mercifully—right after Melanie had been born, when she'd shared a tiny Las Vegas dressing room with thirty other women. She'd learned how to change quickly, with a minimum of movement.

With a smile, Margo shut the door in his face and then turned around.

"If the groom looks anything like his father," she said to Melanie, quickly stripping off her jacket and shirt, "you have found yourself one devil of a good-looking man, sweetheart. I compliment you on your taste."

Melanie found it impossible to think of Lance without a wave of happiness rippling through her. "There's a resemblance."

Shedding her skirt in one fluid motion, Margo wiggled into her dress of soft, shimmering blue, chosen to bring out her eyes as well as the figure she was proud of. "How old is he, anyway?"

Glancing one last time in the mirror, Melanie adjusted the braided gold chain around her neck. A wedding present from Lance. "Lance is thirty."

Margo deftly slipped into the pumps she'd packed in the bottom of the garment bag. "Not him, his father." She turned her back to Joyce. "Joy, do the honors, will you?"

From her cramped position behind the full-length mirror, Joyce reached out and managed to zip Margo's dress up for her. The whole incident, so typically Margo, made her smile. Joyce had grown up living next door to Melanie, her mother and her great-aunt, Elaine. There wasn't a day during that time that she hadn't envied her best friend. Bohemian, unorthodox Margo McCloud had seemed so vital, so dynamic, a box of endless surprises, while her own parents had seemed so mundane and humdrum in comparison.

The fondness had never abated, even after she had become a grown woman.

"Bruce?" Melanie asked in surprise. She paused, thinking. "I don't know."

Glancing in the mirror to make certain everything was in place, Margo retreated, satisfied with her appearance. "He looks more like an older brother than the father of a thirty-year-old man."

Was that a glimmer of interest she saw in her mother's eye? Probably, Melanie decided. There wasn't a man alive Margo McCloud didn't like for one reason or another. The feeling was always returned. Margo made it clear that she enjoyed men's company, enjoyed getting to know them. Not a one of them ever left a relationship with her without becoming a lifelong friend.

She wondered if her mother was just being curious or if there was more to it. "His father was married at a very young age. He and Lance's mother were very much in love. Nature took its course, and Lance's imminent appearance kind of hurried along marriage plans."

She could relate to that, Margo thought. Except that in her case, the result had most definitely not been marriage. Melanie's father had performed his first and last magic trick by making himself disappear out of her life when he learned about her pending appearance.

His loss, Margo thought, looking at her daughter.

"Very romantic. A pity." She stepped out of the room. "There, I'm ready." She turned around quickly for Melanie's inspection. "Fast enough for you?"

"Yes, thank you." Melanie took her mother's arm and started to walk toward the entrance. She saw Joyce signal someone inside. Music began being played in earnest. "What do you mean, it's a pity?"

Margo shrugged carelessly. "That Bruce is married."

Melanie stopped just shy of the double doors. "Oh, but he's not. He's a widower. His wife died in a plane crash years ago."

That put a completely different light on the matter. So good-looking, and free, too. "Hmm."

Melanie didn't know whether to be pleased or ever so slightly concerned. "I know that look." A well-timed warning might be in order. "I think Dad's a wee bit too conservative for you."

The word stopped Margo in her tracks. She stared at Melanie. "Dad?"

It was Melanie's turn to shrug. She'd felt a little awkward about it in the beginning, although secretly it had pleased her.

"Bruce wants me to call him that. I'm trying it on for size." She couldn't help the smile that came. "I have to admit it's nice having someone to call Dad." She'd never had the opportunity to before. There was a time that had bothered her. Perhaps, in a small way, it still did, just a little.

A pang squeezed Margo's heart. "I know it is, baby." It hadn't been easy for her daughter, Margo thought in sympathy, never having had a father to turn to. That had been her fault, though no one had been more surprised than she when Jack had walked out on her. Still she should have known that someone like Jack would never have wanted to be tied down, never have wanted to have a wife, much less a family.

She'd tried her best to make up for it. Maybe she hadn't succeeded as well as she'd thought.

"Hey," Melanie chided. Ever since she'd been a little girl, she'd been able to read her mother the way no one else could. "Don't look like that. I'm just saying that it's nice, after all these years, to have a father, even if I am sharing him." She gave her mother a quick hug. "But I never had to share you with anyone for long, and you were the very best part of my life."

Carefully, because she suddenly needed something to do with her hands, Margo adjusted Melanie's veil about her face. "And you were the best part of mine, baby. The best part of me." The music took on a louder tempo.

Joyce popped her head out into the hall, wondering what was keeping them. "I think the natives are getting restless."

"One second." Without looking in Joyce's direction, Margo held up a single finger. "I would have had more time if the cabdriver had driven the way they do in the movies." A sense of urgency struck Margo, and she took Melanie's hands in hers. A kaleidoscope of memories suddenly flipped over in her mind forming a collage of colors and events, sounds and smells. She loved Melanie more than anyone or anything in this world. Her daughter's happiness was of supreme importance to her. "Do you love him, honey?"

Was that all she wanted to know? The answer was easy. "So much, it hurts."

Margo's eyes held Melanie's. "And does he love you?" Before her daughter could answer, Margo upbraided herself for letting her career get in the way of what was the most important part of her world. "Oh, I wish I'd had time to come sooner, look him over..." Her voice trailed off.

Melanie shook her head, negating the small surge of guilt. She knew her mother couldn't just pick up and leave for a weekend visit. For the last year, she'd been in Greece, hardly a hop, skip and a jump from California. "There's nothing to look over, Mother. He's terrific. And yes, he loves me."

"Then that's all that counts." She kissed Melanie's cheek. "Because if he gives you one bad moment, I'm going to have to kill him, you know."

A smile twitched Melanie's lips. "That should keep him in line nicely." The Wedding March had already begun. Melanie took a deep breath, trying to settle her nerves. Surprisingly, it worked. "Well, they're playing our song."

"No, only yours, baby. They'll never play that song for me."

Margo had resigned herself to that a very long time ago. Marriage had no place in her world. It was better to just go through life expecting little, enjoying whatever there was for however long it lasted. And when some relationship continued, in her estimation, for too long a time, she was the one who tactfully ended it. Before someone ended it for her.

The doors were pushed opened. Music swelled all around them. Holding tightly to the arm wrapped around hers, Margo began to slowly walk down the aisle with her daughter. As with most of her life, this was a break with tradition. Margo was infinitely pleased that Melanie had asked her to give her away, rather than choosing to walk down the aisle alone or having some older man she knew accompany her.

If Melanie had ever belonged to anyone, she'd belonged to her. And now she was going to belong to someone else. And he to her.

Margo could feel her heart swelling with each step she took. She had raised Melanie as best she could, loving every moment of that time. But it had been too short, she thought. Much too short.

"You all right, Mama?" Melanie whispered, inclining her head toward Margo.

Margo nodded. "Fine," she whispered back, "just fine." But she wasn't fine. She wasn't even herself, she thought, annoyed at her own lack of control. "I promised myself I wouldn't cry, and here I am, being so hopelessly traditional I could just scream."

Taking a deep breath, Margo tried to stem the flow that was trickling from the corners of her eyes. After a few seconds, she succeeded. With all her heart she wished she had someone to share this moment with. But for all the friends she had garnered, all the men she felt affection for and who returned the feeling, there was no one for this special moment. No one who had been there from the beginning, to watch a frightened young girl become a mother and somehow manage not to mess up the life of the tiny miracle she'd been entrusted with.

The only person who'd been there, whom she could have shared this with, was gone. Margo thought of Elaine, the woman who had come to her aid, who'd taken her out of a tiny, one-room apartment and a dead-end job as a chorus girl in Las Vegas and brought her into her home and her heart. It was because of Elaine that she had been able to blossom, to be who and what she was today.

"Your aunt Elaine would have loved seeing you like this."

Melanie smiled fondly. Aunt Elaine had been gone almost three years now. The void she left behind would never be filled. But loving Lance had helped a great deal. "I know, Mama, I know."

She didn't want to be maudlin at a time like this. Margo's eyes fixed on the young man standing on the priest's left. "So that's him, eh?"

Melanie's smile lit up her whole body. "Yes, that's him."

"Very nice." Almost there, Margo's eyes strayed to the groom's side of the church. Bruce was in the front row, on the aisle. "The early edition is every bit as handsome as the later one." She gave Melanie's arm a little squeeze. "You two'll make beautiful music and equally beautiful children."

They had come to the front of the church. With a tinge of reluctance that caught her completely off guard, Margo handed her daughter over to a man with kind eyes, then stepped back.

"I see you're not dancing."

Bruce caught the scent of sexy perfume that accompanied the voice and felt a hand on his shoulder. For the second time that day, Bruce was surprised by the same woman.

He looked up to see Margo standing just to his left. The remark was based on the fact that he was sitting alone at a table for eight. Everyone else was on the floor, dancing to the orchestra music.

He shrugged as he felt the hand slide from his shoulder. "I don't really like to dance."

She knew there were men who truly loathed to dance, but there was something in his voice that had Margo not quite buying Bruce's excuse.

She moved to stand in front of him to get a clearer view of his face. "Don't like to dance or don't know how to dance?"

One quick glance told her what she wanted to know. She took his hand in hers, struck by the understated power she felt. She'd always had a fondness for strong men.

"Just as I thought. Come on, let me show you." She was already urging him to his feet. "It's all in the hips, really." To prove it, she placed one of his hands on her hip and moved slowly.

Bruce felt something tighten in his gut even as he found himself being charmed. "What is?" he asked belatedly.

"Rhythm," Margo said, still demonstrating. Gently, as if she were coaxing a fawn out on the ice, she got him to the dance floor. "Let it take you over. Don't think of it as dancing, think of it as moving with the rhythm." Locking her hand with his, she was ready with the first lesson.

When he looked down he saw that her dress seemed to cling to her body like a second skin. The smile on her lips was inviting as her body sealed itself to his. Then she said, "You look like the kind of man who knows just how to move with rhythm." Before he could protest again, Bruce found himself on the floor with Margo, surrounded by other couples. He didn't want to call attention to himself, but he hated feeling like a fool.

She read the reluctance in his eyes, and felt it in his body. He was afraid of being embarrassed. She'd lost the fear of being embarrassed herself years ago. "Don't worry, we'll pretend you're leading."

Her assurance struck him as particularly baseless. "How can I pretend that I'm leading when I don't know what I'm doing?"

The same smile he'd seen on Melanie lit up Margo's eyes. "Simple. Presidents do it all the time."

She winked at him, a lightning-fast flutter of dark brown lashes that had a far greater effect on him than he thought it should. In a last-ditch effort to save himself, he issued her a warning he thought was only fair. "I'm going to step all over your feet."

Oh no, she thought, he wasn't going to get out of having fun that easily.

"My feet can look out for themselves." She jiggled his arm slightly. "Loosen up, Bruce. Just let yourself have a good time."

He thought he was having a good time. "Loosen up?" he echoed. "I wasn't aware that I was 'tight.'"

She looked up into his eyes, wondering if she was making him tense, or if he was just that way in general.

"Oh yes, there's tension all through your shoulders." She brushed her hand lightly across one to make her point. "And judging from the distance from one end to the other, that's a lot of tension."

He took her hand into his, more to immobilize it than to conform to any proper dance position. "I'm out of practice on more than one score." He saw the merriment in her eyes and cocked his head, forgetting to feel like a fish out of water. "Are you flirting with me?"

Amusement danced along cheekbones that a sculptor would have wept over with joy. "If you have to ask, I'm the one out of practice." She relaxed, finding something utterly comforting about being with this man. For the moment she allowed herself to sink into the sensation. "But yes, I'm flirting with you."

They hardly knew each other, he thought. "Why?"

She raised and lowered her slim shoulders. "Why does a woman usually flirt?" He underestimated himself about the dancing, she thought. He was dancing very nicely.

The smile on his lips was self-deprecating. "I said I was out of practice."

Margo enumerated the reasons for him. "A woman flirts with a man to be complimented. Or because she's with a good-looking man and would like his attention. She flirts because it feels good. Or to be friendly because that's her way."

They danced by Lance and Melanie. Margo felt a slight tug on her heart. She'd encouraged Melanie to be independent since she'd taken her first step, but she'd never seen how well the lesson had been learned until this moment. Melanie was all grown-up and on her own.

"Or maybe," Margo said quietly, watching the younger couple dance, "because her only daughter's just gotten married and she's feeling a little world-weary, a little lost."

Bruce waited until the pause drew itself out into silence. "Is this where I'm supposed to choose one of the above?"

Rousing herself, Margo smiled as she nodded. "Yes, this would be the logical place."

"The last one?" He thought it was a safe guess.

She'd opened up a little more of herself than she'd meant and now retreated. Light laughter filled the air. "Wrong. To be friendly," she told him. Purposely Margo maneuvered Bruce so that her back was to her daughter. Getting misty twice in one day was twice too many. "I like people, Bruce. I like them to like me. With men, that means a little flirting."

Across the floor Melanie watched their progress with amusement and a touch of concern. She liked Bruce. Liked him a great deal. A man like that was completely unarmed when it came to someone like her mother. Unarmed and unprepared.

She raised her eyes to her new husband. "My mother is dancing with your father. Think I should warn him about her?"

Lance would have hated to admit it at one time, but he and his father were a lot alike. Or had been, until Melanie had entered his life. His father deserved a chance at mining that kind of treasure.

Lance shook his head. "If she's anything like you, she'll be the best thing that ever happened to him."

The compliment warmed her, but it didn't dispel her concern. That was just the problem. At bottom, her mother wasn't like her.

Melanie bit her lower lip as she watched the pair move in slow circles on one tiny section of the dance floor. *Go easy on him, Mama.*

Chapter Two

Margo raised her head to look up at the man who managed to extend an attitude of respectfulness toward her even while he held her close enough to make her pulse beat in time to the music. She knew without being told that Bruce Reed was a shy man. A hundred years or so ago, he might have even been referred to as a courtly man.

There was a lot to be said for courtly, she mused, enjoying the feel of his arms around her.

The thought occurred to her that chivalry and manners had definitely been underrated in the past few decades.

Or maybe, a small voice whispered to her, it might be that she had gotten just the least bit weary of life in the fast lane. Bruce Reed, with his reluctant, shy smile, his kind eyes and polite ways was like a breath of fresh air to her.

Mentally, Margo shrugged away the choices. Whatever the cause of her feelings, it was nice, dancing like this with the tall, handsome stranger fate and the state of California had linked her to. Drifting with the music, she let herself just enjoy the moment. That had been her credo for the last twenty some odd years. Enjoy the moment, because the next one might just come by and knock you on your seat.

Margo moved her hand up along his arm, resting it lightly on his jacket. Even so, she could detect the hard muscle that was just beneath. Handsome and strong, she thought. That was unusual in a man over thirty.

The smile she directed Bruce's way was slow, deep and, some had told her, lethal. His unspoken reaction to it pleased her, as well.

She studied his face. "How old are you?"

Leery about where this was going, he asked, "Why?"

She shrugged, her shoulder brushing against him. It was a nice sensation. Going with it, Margo laid her head against his chest. "You don't look old enough to have a son like Lance."

This was nice, he thought, surprised by her familiarity and his own reaction to it. They were hardly moving on the floor and yet it felt nice. His cheek brushed ever so slightly against the top of her head. The vague tingle he felt made him forget that he hated to dance. "Thank you," he told her. "I can honestly say I return the compliment."

Margo raised her head. A smile curved her mouth. "I don't look old enough to have a son like Lance?" she asked, teasing him. "I'm not."

That had gotten twisted somehow. "No, I meant—"

"I know what you meant," she told him, taking him off the hook he seemed destined to impale himself on, although she had to admit, he made being flustered seem almost adorable. "That I don't look old enough to be Melanie's mother. And it's a very nice compliment."

It took Bruce a moment to focus on the conversation. The way she had looked up at him had temporarily blown all thoughts out of his mind, filling the space with her image. He'd never seen eyes quite so blue before, or quite so compelling. *Hypnotic* was the word for it, he amended. And for the lady, as well. It was like holding solidified quick-silver in his arms. There for the moment, but not for long.

Lance's new mother-in-law, he caught himself thinking, was one hell of a remarkable woman.

"It's not a compliment," Bruce corrected her. She was probably on the receiving end of a dozen a day. He had no intention of getting involved in some sort of unofficial competition. "It's an observation. You really do look more like Melanie's sister than her mother."

She'd heard it before, but it wasn't something she was about to become tired of anytime soon. As time went by, she cherished the compliment more and more.

With a stately nod, she replied, "I had her when I was eleven."

Her face was so straight, her voice so solemn, Bruce didn't know whether she was pulling his leg, or, fueled by champagne, revealing a deep, dark confidence to him. There were women in his acquaintance, his sister, Bess, being one of them, who couldn't take more than a few sips of anything remotely alcoholic without feeling compelled to make a clean breast of any and all past sins and transgressions, whether minor or major. He had no idea which category Margo fell into, although he had his suspicions.

The best way to handle this, he decided, was gracefully. He just hoped he remembered how. "You're that much older than she is?"

The guileless remark caught her off guard. And then she laughed, completely charmed by a man she could tell wasn't trying to be charming. Despite the very handsome figure he cut in his tailor-made tuxedo, Bruce Reed was very obviously just struggling not to commit any unforgivable social error on this very important day in his son's life.

Here was a man, she decided, she'd really love to spend some time with.

"Oh, Bruce, you are good for me." When her eyes swept over him, Bruce felt a good deal warmer than he had just a moment earlier. "The truth is, I'm seventeen years older than Melanie." Margo paused, quickly subtracting the months that separated her birthday from her daughter's. "Seventeen and a half, to be precise."

The figure struck very close to home. It occurred to Bruce that they had an unofficial bond, Margo and he, both becoming parents before they reached their twentieth birthday.

"My wife was almost nineteen when Lance was born. She was five months older than I was." He was unaware of the fond smile that took possession of his lips as he allowed himself, for the space of a heartbeat, to be transported to another time and place.

But Margo wasn't. What she didn't understand was why his smile sent such a ripple of bittersweet longing through her.

"I always told her I had a fondness for older women," Bruce said. A ream of memories tumbled through his mind and he laughed. "She never cared for that remark." And then he sobered slightly as the sadness, even after all this time, came to embrace him. "But she never got to be old enough for that to become an issue." And then he realized he probably sounded as if he were rambling. Margo deserved an explanation. "My wife died while she was still very young."

And he was still in love with her. Margo was touched by the sentiment she saw in his eyes.

She supposed that the appropriate response to his revelation was something along the lines of offering her condolences, but somehow she had a feeling he didn't want to hear empty words from a stranger. They wouldn't change what was.

Instead she told him what she felt. "Your wife was a very lucky woman."

Surprised, Bruce raised a brow. How could a woman who died too young to see the autumn of her years, too young to see her child reach his destiny, be considered lucky? "What makes you say that?"

"The way your face lit up when you mentioned her." She couldn't help but envy Lance's mother. Though gone, the woman still retained her husband's love. It said a lot about the woman. And a lot about the man who loved her. "The most important ingredient in a person's life is love, and it appears to me that she had it in abundance."

Yes, he thought. Ellen had. He couldn't remember a day when he hadn't loved her. It seemed to him that they had always been together, right from the very beginning. Whatever had come before that time was a blur. Just like life without her had become.

As they turned on the floor, he caught a whiff of Margo's fragrance again. It sharpened his senses and he smiled at the woman in his arms. "You're very perceptive."

Margo took her due without vanity. Perception was closely interwoven with her other survival skills. "So I've been told."

She was open rather than coy. It was an honest trait. He valued honesty a great deal. "Well, you're certainly not shy and retiring."

Oh, but I am. The thought came to her from nowhere, standing like a lost soul in the dark. *It's just something that I can't allow to take over anymore. Or even be noticed.* Very carefully, Margo kept her thoughts from registering on her face. She'd become very good at that over the years.

"You know my daughter," she reminded him lightly. "Would you really have expected me to be?"

She had a point. They were very alike, mother and daughter. And yet he detected that there were minor differences. For one, Margo was far more worldly than her daughter. And perhaps, he mused, less apt to be hurt. "No, but I have to admit that I didn't expect anyone quite so effervescent, either."

"Effervescent?" Delighted, she laughed lightly. "Oh,

my dear Mr. Reed, I'm in fairly low gear now.'' She looked toward Melanie and felt that same tightening of her throat she'd felt when she'd walked into the change room to see her daughter in her wedding gown for the first time. ''I think that realizing things just refuse to remain the same, no matter how much you'd really like them to, is responsible for subduing me.''

Because the same bittersweetness resided within him, Bruce recognized the signs. The feeling of kinship grew as the music around them faded. Bruce hardly noticed. He was hearing another melody, one within his head.

Continuing to move to this silent music, he tried to tease her mood away. ''If this is low gear, then heaven help the man who gets you in high gear.''

He really was very sweet, Margo thought. And whether he realized it or not, he was doing tremendous things for her ego. She needed that right now, as the loneliness insisted on closing in no matter how hard she tried to block it.

''Heaven has very little to do with it. Or me.'' Her wink was positively bawdy, Bruce thought, feeling its effect as it simmered over his long frame. ''Or so my father said the last time I saw him.''

Looking into her eyes, he almost thought he saw sadness there. But everything in her manner belied the discovery. He had to be mistaken.

''Which was?'' he prodded.

If she closed her eyes, Margo could still see the cold dark look of disapproval, of condemnation in Egan McCloud's green eyes as he ordered her to leave. No instrument known to man could have begun to measure the depth of that cold.

She took a breath before answering, her smile never faltering. She'd begun to show at four months. By five, her father no longer believed that it was a weight problem.

"Four months before that beautiful young woman in the bridal dress was born."

As she spoke, Bruce could feel her body stiffening. It was infinitesimal, but he was positive he detected it. Having gone through his own schism with Lance, he would have thought his sympathies would have been with her father. They weren't. "You haven't seen him since then?"

She shook her head, wishing the memory didn't hurt so much. She was a grown woman, for heaven's sake, with a grown child of her own. When did she finally cease regretting that she'd never been allowed to be Daddy's little girl, not even for the space of five minutes?

"Not alive." She strove to say the words without emotion. She'd returned for the funeral. And never shed a tear. She'd refused to. "He wanted nothing to do with me." The shrug was careless, as a creamy white shoulder rose and fell beneath his glance. "He was a very God-fearing man, and I think he saw me as a terrible failing on his part."

She believed that, Bruce realized. His sympathies stacked themselves completely on her side. He knew what it was like, aching for someone's acceptance. In his case, it had been his son's that he had sought. Lance's acceptance and his forgiveness. Both had been a long time in coming.

Not that he blamed Lance. Feeling as if he'd been cast adrift after his wife died, he'd left Lance to be raised by Bess. He hadn't realized how his leaving had affected his son.

Unconsciously, Bruce gathered her a little closer to him as they danced. "I might be out of place saying this, but seems to me that your father would have done a lot better by you as well as himself if he were a God-loving man instead."

The smile she offered him reminded Bruce of fireflies lighting up a June sky. And, if he didn't know any better, he would have sworn there was a tinge of gratitude in her eyes.

For a tongue-tied man, he certainly did know how to turn a phrase, Margo thought. "For Melanie's sake, I do hope Lance takes after you."

The remark struck a chord that had, until recently, been very painful. "Lance went out of his way for a long time to be the exact opposite of me." Bruce placed the blame where it belonged. With him. "I wasn't a very good father."

Margo swept past his remorse, a spring breeze traveling through a ripening orchard. There was nothing so useless as regret over things that couldn't be changed. "I'm sure that if there's any basis for your feelings, there were extenuating circumstances."

There were very far-reaching, painful circumstances. But this was Lance's wedding. It wasn't a time to talk about death and the way it had burned out his heart, leaving only ashes in its place.

"Tell me, are you always this broad-minded?"

She inclined her head. "Some people say it's my best feature."

Holding her close to him, Bruce wasn't so sure about that. If asked, it would have been difficult for him to say just exactly what Margo's best feature was. She was beautiful in a warm, welcoming sort of way rather than in the precise features of an ice princess.

Looks weren't supposed to matter. He'd learned a long time ago that transient outer beauty was hardly important, but he had to admit Melanie's mother was a feast for the eyes. And her manner, open, warm, sensually charming, enhanced that feast tenfold.

"I wouldn't exactly say that," he told her.

She liked the way he smiled. "Oh?" Her eyes delved straight into his soul. "And what would you say. Exactly?"

Compliments really weren't his forte. Neither was conversation, but he had the heartening feeling that he was at least holding his own. "That I have the comfort of knowing that I wouldn't be the only tongue-tied man around you."

But she shook her head at his assessment of himself. "For a 'tongue-tied' man, you're doing very well, Bruce. And for what it's worth, I really do hope Lance is exactly like you."

The compliment, sincerely rendered, touched him. It had been a long time since he'd thought of himself and Lance as a unit.

"Thanks to Melanie, I'll get to find out if he is or not firsthand." He saw the question enter Margo's eyes. "It's because of Melanie that Lance and I reconciled. From what I hear, she kept after him about it, making it easier for me when we finally did talk." He could see a great deal of Margo in her daughter. "You did a wonderful job raising her."

She hadn't raised her so much as just been there to oversee the process. Melanie had never really needed guidance. She was inherently savvy, inherently good. Other than a bout with the croup, Margo had never given her even a moment's concern. She'd always been the kind of daughter every mother dreamed about.

But Margo had no intentions of playing the gushing mother and boring Bruce to tears. She gave him the short, unannotated version. "I had help."

Bruce made the most logical assumption. "Your husband?"

Husband, now there was a joke. Margo shook her head. "My aunt."

"We have that in common, I guess. Lance was raised by his aunt Bess, my sister. That's her over there," he said, pointing her out, "dancing. I'll introduce you to her later. She took over with Lance when my wife died."

If he was going to be family, Margo decided, there would be no secrets. Any shame attached to the situation had long since been burned away in the glow of Melanie's smile.

"Melanie's father did a very impressive vanishing act as soon as he knew that fifteen minutes of pleasure resulted in something that was going to require an eighteen-year commitment."

The revelation surprised him. Bruce couldn't picture any man in his right mind walking away from Margo. "I take it he was blind?"

She laughed softly. "No, just heartless and stupid." Whenever she thought of Jack, there was nothing there anymore. No pain, no anger, nothing. It had taken her a long time to arrive at that juncture. "To be blind he wouldn't have been able to see his way out of my life, which he did. Quickly." At the time it had taken her breath away just how quickly. Taken her breath and her heart.

"But Jack was very stupid because he missed out on a hell of an experience. I wouldn't have traded being Melanie's mother, not even a minute of it, for anything in the world, including a fantastic marriage."

She'd talked enough about herself, she thought, steering the conversation onto a new road. "Which, by the way, I'm sure Melanie and Lance are going to have. She's crazy about him."

That was very evident and it made Bruce's heart glad. "And he about her. We both are. Lance is convinced she's brought out the best in him, and, even though I've only known her a few short months, I certainly can't argue with that."

Melanie was surprised that neither her mother nor Bruce seemed to notice her as she came up to them. But the fact that they were still dancing told her that they were well on their way to slipping into a world of their own.

One look at Bruce and she knew that her mother was weaving her magic again. Maybe this time, Melanie hoped, she'd get tangled in the threads herself.

But that wasn't her mother's style.

Melanie placed a hand on each of their shoulders, securing their attention. Bruce looked surprised to see her, her mother only looked amused. "Hey, did anyone tell you two that the music stopped two minutes ago?"

Margo merely smiled at her daughter. There was music and then there was music. Melanie would learn, she thought. Someday. "Just the music you can hear, dear." Very slowly, she disengaged her hand from Bruce's. "But we don't want to give them anything to talk about, do we?"

Bruce found himself reluctant to break contact. He slipped his arm around her shoulders, escorting Margo from the floor. "That depends on what they're saying."

Melanie looked from Bruce to her mother. Just the slightest flutter of uncertainty traveled through her before disappearing. She'd never interfered in her mother's life before. She owed everything to her mother, and there was no one she loved more dearly, except for Lance. But Bruce was her father-in-law now. More like a father, really, than just someone the law claimed was related to her. Though she'd known him only four months, she felt protective of him. At bottom, Bruce was a sweet man who might misunderstand her mother's ways. She didn't want to see either of them hurt.

Melanie took her mother's hand in hers, making her apology to Bruce. "Can I steal my mother for a minute, Dad?"

The question amused him. Margo wasn't his to give away. "I have a distinct feeling that your mother is very much her own woman." The smile he received told him Margo appreciated his recognizing that fact. "She'll only be stolen if she wants to be. What someone else has to say about it doesn't enter into the picture."

Margo's smile widened. And grew sexier, in Bruce's estimation.

Oh boy, Melanie thought. She took her mother's hand and tugged ever so gently. "Just a minute," she promised again.

This wasn't like Melanie, Margo thought. Her daughter looked almost worried as she led her off. "Okay, out with it," Margo ordered when they were barely out of Bruce's earshot. "What's wrong?"

Where to begin? Heaven knew, Melanie didn't want to hurt her mother's feelings. But she didn't want to see Bruce's feelings hurt, either. She plunged in, beginning with a declaration. "Mama, you know I love you."

Years of experience warned Margo what was coming next. "There's a lecture attached to that proclamation, isn't there?"

This was all virgin territory for Melanie. She wouldn't presume to tell her mother what to do. She wet her lips. "Not a lecture, but..."

Margo didn't need subtitles to tell her what was going on. "You're afraid I'm going to lay waste to Lance's father."

Melanie took her mother's hand between her own. "Not exactly waste, but—"

Gently slipping her hand away, Margo cupped Melanie's cheek. Was she really worried? "Sweetheart, he's a very charming man without meaning to be, which makes him even more so. But charming or not, all we're doing is just swapping old in-law stories."

Melanie arched an eyebrow. The word *old* had never had anything remotely to do with her mother. "Neither one of you is an old anything."

Margo's eyes sparkled. "That's what makes swapping so much fun."

Maybe, Melanie thought, Bruce could do with a dose of her mother. A small dose to make him feel vital again, but not enough to drown him. "What else are you going to swap?"

"Well, not clothes," Margo teased, slipping her arm through Melanie's, "he's way too tall." Margo studied Melanie's face. She *was* concerned. The realization took her slightly aback. "Honey, just what are you worried about?"

There had never been any lies between them, not even half truths. Melanie couldn't set a precedent now. "Bruce isn't exactly a sophisticated, experienced man as far as women are concerned, Mama. I don't want to see him hurt."

The fact that Melanie's loyalty lay with someone else stung her a little before she banked it down. Her smile remained intact as she asked, "How about me?"

Melanie laughed, giving her mother's hand a quick, firm squeeze. "You can handle yourself. You always have."

That was the price she paid for being strong, Margo thought. No one thought for a moment that she might be the one who could be hurt.

Which was, she reminded herself quickly with no patience for her momentary lapse, just the way she wanted it and just the way she always kept it. Never mind that it wasn't true. That wasn't anyone's business but hers.

She winked at Melanie. "I promise not to skewer any vital, irreplaceable part of Mr. Bruce Reed, including his heart. How's that?"

Melanie's expression softened, guilt lightly flicking a finger at her conscience. "I didn't mean to sound judgmental, Mama, but he doesn't even date. He leads a very straight and narrow life. The man won't even let himself be fixed up by any of his married friends."

A challenge, thought Margo. She always loved a challenge, especially one that was so good-looking. "Then it's about time he had a little fun, don't you think?"

Melanie looked at her dubiously. "A little, yes, but—"

Margo raised one hand in a solemn pledge. "I promise not to lead him into Sodom or Gomorrah for at least the remainder of the afternoon."

This time guilt not only flicked Melanie, it pinched. Remorse was instant. "I'm sorry, Mama, I didn't mean to hurt your feelings."

The tables turned immediately. Not for the world would Margo give her daughter one moment's grief or concern. "You could never hurt my feelings, pet. Have you forgotten, I've got a hide as tough as a rhino?"

But Melanie saw through that. "It wasn't your 'hide' I was thinking about."

Margo redirected Melanie's attention to her groom. "And it shouldn't be my anything that's on your mind at all. Not when you have that drop-dead-gorgeous man of yours promising to love and cherish you for the rest of his natural life." She cocked her head, struggling to keep a grin from her lips. "Don't you two have a honeymoon to go to?"

Melanie and Lance had discussed that and decided to put it off until they could afford to go to someplace memorable. "We're not planning on going on a honeymoon until sometime later."

Margo already knew that. She'd called and taken Joyce into her confidence. It was Joyce who'd secretly packed their luggage. "Take it from me, later has a habit of either slipping away or being used for something else. Go now, you won't regret it."

"I'm afraid that we ca—"

Allowing herself a dramatic flourish, Margo produced two airline tickets from her beaded purse. "Two tickets to Hawaii and a two-week reservation at the best hotel on Oahu."

Overwhelmed, Melanie could only stare at the tickets in her mother's hand. "Mother, you didn't."

Margo pressed the tickets into her hand. "The airline and hotel people seem to think I did."

Lance joined them, slipping his arm around Melanie's waist. He noticed the stunned expression on her face. "Everything all right?" He kissed her temple. "I got lonely."

He couldn't have been better if she'd handpicked him, Margo thought. Pleased, she took each of their hands in hers and held them for a moment, her heart brimming. "Oh, God, Melanie, he is perfect."

Recovering, Melanie held up the tickets. "Mother's sending us to Hawaii for our honeymoon."

Coming to grips with his surprise, Lance began to demur. Margo recognized pride when she saw it and quickly headed it off. "It's a wedding present. Two tickets to Oahu, first class, plus you'll be staying at the best hotel, in the bridal suite."

That had to have set her back a lot. Lance shook his head. "Mrs.—I mean Ms.—" Neither term seemed appropriate. He took a breath. "We can't—"

"Call me Margo," Margo told him. "We're going to be an informal family. And I certainly can't go, so you have to. You're the only bridal couple I see in the room."

Lance tried again, having the sinking feeling that the effort was doomed to failure. He already knew where arguing with Melanie got him. Nowhere. And he had a strong suspicion that it was a hereditary trait. "This is too generous."

Money was only good for the happiness it could generate. There was no way she was going to let either one of them turn her gift down. "I have only one daughter, Lance. And, as of one o'clock this afternoon, only one son. I can't think of anyone I'd rather spend my money on than the two of you. Besides, you can't refuse a wedding gift, it's bad luck."

Melanie placed one hand on her hip, suppressing a smile. When she was a little girl, her mother used to get her to do things by telling her that if she refused, it was bad luck. There was always a legend or fable that reflected the situation attached. She was fourteen before she realized that her mother had made all the fables up. "Another legend I don't know about?"

Nostalgia surged through Margo. "As a matter of fact, yes."

Lance opened his mouth, but Melanie stopped him. "Don't bother. Nobody's ever managed to talk Mama out of anything once she makes up her mind."

He'd kind of figured that out on his own. "I wasn't going to talk her out of it, I was just going to say thank you." Lance looked at Margo, then with a smile, added, "Mom."

There had to be something in the air today, some allergen that kept making her eyes tear up. Margo blinked twice, struggling not to let a single drop slip down her cheek. "Don't mention it," she murmured, embracing him.

Chapter Three

The car with Lance and Melanie in it pulled slowly away from the curb. The sound of the engine was drowned out by the cheers and raised voices, all attempting to outshout one another as they tried to make their own best wishes heard above the rest.

The din seemed to swirl around Margo like leaves caught up in the rush of a breeze, chasing one another in an eternally forward-moving circle.

Margo drew away from the edge of the crowd. She felt oddly removed from what was going on, a spectator who had just happened upon a scene and had yet to become a part of it. There was no denying that her heart was full to overflowing with happiness for her daughter, but at the same time, there was a downside to that joy. A sense of exclusion embraced her, making her feel strangely alone. More alone than she'd felt since she'd walked out of her father's house all those years ago.

Annoyed with herself, with these emotions that insisted on roller-coastering through her, Margo struggled to regain control.

Oblivious to the people around her, she didn't realize at first that the handkerchief at her elbow was being silently offered to her. When she did, she raised her eyes to look at the owner. It didn't really surprise her that it was Bruce.

"Thought you might need this." When she didn't attempt to accept the handkerchief, he added, "It's clean."

Her mouth curved. "I'm sure your practice of hygiene is beyond reproach, Bruce, but I really don't need a handkerchief."

Yeah, you do, he thought, but rather than press the point, he pocketed the offering. Maybe she needed to deny her need more than she needed to wipe away the tears shimmering in her eyes.

"My mistake," he allowed gallantly. With adroit ability that came from implementing compromises at business meetings, he nudged the conversation along a different path. "That was a very nice thing you did for them, sending Melanie and Lance off on an all-expense-paid honeymoon."

She merely lifted a shoulder in mute response, then let it drop, her eyes straining to retain sight of the disappearing car until the last possible moment. It was only money, thankfully the least of her concerns these days.

"I tried to do the same thing," he confessed, a would-be contender sharing a mutual, though unattained, goal, "but got turned down. Lance has this thing about being his own man. I can see where it'd be harder for him to refuse you. I mean—"

He didn't want Margo to think that he meant he thought she was pushy. And when he played the fragment over again in his head, this time it sounded suspiciously like a come-on line. Hell, but he really was out of practice talking to women.

He smiled ruefully when she looked at him, a patient question in her eyes. "Do you always make men feel as if their tongues have gotten too big for their mouths?"

She laughed then, a deep throaty laugh that he thought had a touch of relief to it.

Margo felt relieved that she could still laugh, despite the hollow feeling taking root.

"No, not usually."

Bruce could only shake his head. It was just as he thought. "Must be me, then." He shoved his hands into his pockets. Maybe he was the one who was being pushy, but in his estimation, it was for a worthy cause. "I don't usually do this, but, um, would you like to go somewhere for a cup of coffee or something?"

Was he trying to ask her out? Amusement began to nudge away the sadness. Margo looked down at the dress she was wearing, then raised her eyes to take in his tuxedo. "I think we might be just a little overdressed for a coffee shop."

She had a point. Looking at her addled his brain a little. He'd spent half the reception dancing with her and could honestly say he didn't remember when he'd had a better time in recent years.

"A drink, then." Bruce turned, nodding toward the building behind them where the reception had been held. All around them, people were breaking up into groups and couples, bound for the parking lot and home, or perhaps to continue the celebration with an evening on the town. "At the lounge downstairs," he prompted. "You look like you might need a little company." Before she got any wrong ideas about his motives, he quickly added, "Strictly platonic, of course. In-law to in-law."

He was like a fish out of water, Margo thought. A very cute, cuddly fish. Why hadn't he been snapped up by one of the women in his circle yet?

"Platonic, eh?" She snapped her fingers like someone who had just missed an opportunity. "I guess there go all my plans of having my way with you."

The sound of her laughter slipped under his skin, arousing him before he could steel himself. He banked down the reaction that had no place within the good deed he was trying to accomplish.

"Not that I'm averse to stimulating conversation, or stimulating anything," she put in, her eyes beginning to reclaim their sparkle, "but what makes you say that I need company?"

Instead of answering, Bruce cupped her chin in his hand and raised it slightly. Taking out his handkerchief again, he lightly dabbed at the corner of her eye where one renegade tear had refused to obey and remain confined.

For one very long moment, as he touched her, her eyes held his. Something warm slipped around her, like a protective embrace. But the next moment, it was gone. Embarrassed, Margo drew back her head.

"Just a hunch." With a shrug, his eyes still on hers, Bruce tucked the handkerchief back into his pocket. "Maybe it's me who needs the company."

He was attempting to be gallant. When was the last time a man had been nothing more than gallant to her? So long, she wasn't quite sure if she remembered.

Her smile was light, teasing, as she slipped her arm through his. "Well, far be it from me to deny a handsome man his platonic request."

She made it sound as if she was given to fielding platonic requests all the time. Bruce sincerely doubted, as they walked back into the Renaissance Building, that Margo McCloud met very many men who desired only a platonic relationship with her. Not once they heard her lusty laughter.

She should have had twelve children, all girls, Margo thought with a pang that bordered on longing as she hung up the telephone.

Better yet, she should have had Melanie cloned as a little

girl. That way she'd be assured of revisiting this wonderful feeling periodically.

Since business was slow at Dreams of Yesterday, where she'd been working every day now for two weeks, helping out until Melanie returned, Margo took a moment to reflect. It was a silly thought, but not without its merits or its reasons. Her life had grown tremendously since she'd left that small Texas town with one suitcase, a swollen belly and a blank future before her. When she had ridden the bus out of Hemp, she'd been an unwed, pregnant teenage dropout, hitting the lowest point of her young life.

But even though she'd been frightened and emotionally battered, she hadn't surrendered to defeat. Hadn't allowed herself to become just another statistic in a world that held on to its losers as tightly as it did to its winners. She'd gotten her diploma, and then a degree in languages. Now she traveled the world, teaching languages to Americans who found themselves working in foreign countries. She had friends on all the major continents and could literally get along anywhere.

But all her accomplishments paled beside the triumph she'd reached in having Melanie. In keeping Melanie rather than giving her up. The very best part of her life had always revolved around Melanie, around raising her and making the promise within a newborn become a very positive reality.

God, but she fervently wished she could do it all over again.

Joyce came up behind her, placing the stack of newly acquired autographed celebrity stills on the counter beside the telephone. In the foreground, a very satisfied customer made her way out of the shop Joyce and Melanie partnered in Bedford.

"Good news?" she asked hesitantly, peering at Margo's expression.

With a self-deprecating smile, Margo turned to her

daughter's best friend, a young woman she'd known since before Joy had said her first word.

"Yes, as a matter of fact it is." Joy was looking at her oddly. "Why?"

Joyce made a noncommittal sound as she shrugged self-consciously. "You had a very strange look on your face when I walked up."

That would be the nostalgia, Margo thought. "Mothers do that when they suddenly realize that they have fully grown daughters who have lives of their own." She rallied before she could slip back into that wistful mood again. "Speaking of whom, that was Melanie on the phone. She and Lance are coming back tomorrow." Her voice began to pick up speed, reflecting her heightened energy as she simultaneously made plans and talked. "That means I'll be out of your hair soon." Which studio was Jason Riveria working for these days, Margo wondered, distracted. He'd have a lock on those harem props she needed, she was sure of it.

"Margo, I wouldn't have known what to do if you hadn't been here to help out." If Joyce had her way, Melanie and Margo would handle all the sales while she buried herself in the back with the accounting details. "I'm not very good with people."

Roused by the distress she heard, Margo looked at the young woman. She placed her arm around Joy's shoulder, drawing her closer. The trouble with Joy was she had a poor self-image, and that was all her mother's doing. Or lack of doing, she amended.

"Yes, you are, you're just quieter than I am. But then, most people are." She winked, as if that was a secret instead of a given. "You know, I've been thinking…"

Joyce didn't know whether to be wary or let herself go along with whatever was coming. Probably the latter. Not that she had much of a choice if Margo's idea involved her.

To her knowledge, no one had ever been able to stop Melanie's mother when she got rolling.

Joyce's grin had a touch of nervousness to it. "Is this where I say, uh-oh?"

Margo laughed, giving Joy an affectionate squeeze. "No, but Lance might when he realizes what sort of a family he married into."

The sound of her laughter was the first thing he heard as Bruce entered the shop.

It seemed fitting. It was that sound, flittering in and out of his brain these past two weeks, that had brought him here this afternoon. He'd come here on his day off rather than getting to the myriad of things that he'd been letting pile up in his personal life.

The fact that he had, that he caught himself thinking about Margo at unlikely moments, surprised him. If he didn't count that incredibly annoying woman he'd been forced to deal with at the local courthouse the one time he'd gotten a traffic ticket, no woman had ever intruded into his thoughts beyond the moment. The only one who had ever occupied his mind for more than a fleeting moment was Ellen.

Margo was nothing like Ellen.

Maybe that was the reason.

The reason he was here, he insisted silently, was just to see how she was doing. When he'd dropped her off here after the reception, she'd told him that she was fine. He would have taken her at her word, but the moonlight had played along her skin, urging him to take one last, lingering look. When he did, there'd been something about her, something in her eyes, that had made him doubt the validity of her assertion.

He just wanted to make sure she was all right, he told himself again. After all, she was Lance's mother-in-law, and although there was no legal term for the bond that he now shared with her, that didn't mean there wasn't one.

Like it or not they were family, and his was small enough for him to take a personal interest in each member, now that he had his priorities straight and had lived through his period of atonement.

Margo turned toward the doorway, alerted by the musical chimes that someone had entered the store.

If she was surprised to see Bruce walking in, she didn't show it. Instead, she came around the small counter, her hands outstretched in a warm greeting, a smile unfurling on her lips like a flag at first light.

The man had a gift, she thought, for appearing just at the right moment. She gave him a quick, enthusiastic hug. "Just the man I need."

He didn't know whether to be flattered or braced. He suspected that a great many people felt that way in her presence. Finding himself disengaged from a hug he was just beginning to enjoy, he looked down at Margo and raised one eyebrow in silent query. "Oh?"

"Yes." The single word was fueled with an incredible amount of feeling. Had Melanie been there, she would have told him he was in for trouble. Taking a step back, she looked him over quickly, like a tailor wondering if the suit he'd made would fit his customer. "Tell me, Bruce, do you have a strong back?"

"My back?" he echoed uncertainly. It wasn't a question he expected to be asked. Just what was it this woman had in mind?

"Yes." The casual clothes he had on strongly reinforced the impression she'd gotten at the reception when she'd danced with him. The man looked to be made of solid muscle. But not all shortcomings were evident to the eye. "No old football injuries or anything?"

He turned, watching her as she circled him. "I never played football."

That was hard to believe. Margo came full circle to face him again. "How about baseball?"

"A little." She was making him uneasy. It was time to find out where she was headed with this conversation. "Margo, what are you getting at, and should we be having this conversation in front of people?" He glanced toward Joyce who looked about as lost as to Margo's meaning as he felt.

Joy was far too slight to be of any use to her at the moment. "Joyce isn't people, she's like another daughter." Her smile was wicked as she read his thoughts. "And besides, I'm only trying to find out if you're up to moving some furniture for me, not any acrobatics in bed."

"Furniture?" Was that it? Relief reared its head, but there were questions on its heels. One question brought with it interest sharp enough to give him pause. "Are you moving back to the area?"

Her mind busy with logistics and phone calls she had yet to make, it took Margo a second to regroup and assimilate the direction his question was going. "Oh, no, I never take furniture with me. It ties you down too much." Her attachments were to places, to friends, not to anything that could be stored in a building or a box. "Whatever I own is right upstairs." She raised her eyes toward the ceiling. "I lived with Aunt Elaine while Melanie was growing up. When my career began to take me to different places, I just left everything behind. It's much easier that way."

"No suitcases stuffed with clothes?" He couldn't bring himself to believe that a woman with Margo's figure would be careless about what she wore.

He had her there. But clothes didn't tie her down the way other possessions would. "Oh, well, clothes come under the heading of necessities. I wouldn't get very much done if I had to teach naked, now, would I?"

He tried, without much success, not to dwell on that image. "Depended on what lesson you were working on," he murmured.

Now why did a statement so casually shy cause her pulse

to jump a notch? He did have a way about him, she thought. A very unstudied, sexy way. Delicately, she let the topic drop. "Actually, I was thinking of Melanie and Lance's place."

There was a glint in her eyes. He caught the concerned expression on Joy's face. He took it as a warning. The other woman knew Margo far better than he did.

"Am I going to have to sit down for this?" he wanted to know.

"Well, eventually," she conceded. "Once you get tired."

He had a feeling that he was going to reach that condition just listening to her. "Exactly what is it you have in mind?"

As far as he knew, the apartment Lance and Melanie had rented was already furnished with a composite of her furniture, his furniture and what they whimsically referred to as "their" furniture. The latter consisted solely of an oblong sofa they had bought a week before the wedding.

"It's very simple, really." To Margo everything was simple. Some things just took a little longer to get to that state than others. "I want to arrange a surprise for them."

He didn't know her well enough to know if her surprises were considered good or not by the recipients. "What kind of a surprise?"

Margo had no idea just how much Bruce knew about her daughter's background. Playing it unusually safe, she gave him a thumbnail sketch.

"Melanie was practically raised on the lots of different movie studios. That's how the store evolved." She gestured carelessly at walls that were covered with framed, personally autographed photos and a showroom that was arranged to look like her aunt's parlor, filled with memorabilia. "Aunt Elaine worked as a makeup artist and costume designer for two of the major studios for over fifty years. She never met a person she didn't like and who didn't like her."

The wholesale declaration amused him. "Your aunt was Will Rogers?"

"Better. Will Rogers didn't know how to put on make-up."

"Thank God for small favors," he murmured under his breath, only to have her sensual laugh surround him. It galvanized his attention to her lips and to what she was saying, among other things.

"Anyway, I thought it might be fun for her—and Lance—if I—we," she amended with a penetrating look, "—decorated their bedroom like a harem." As she spoke, she made quick, abbreviated notes to herself, ideas coming to her with the speed of a Thoroughbred racing to the finish line of his first Kentucky Derby. "And their living room like the interior of a medieval castle—"

He couldn't help himself. "And their kitchen?"

The look in her eyes was raw sensuality before it receded. He wondered if she knew how devastating she was. The next moment he wondered if there were any bigger fools around than him. Margo McCloud was aware of every move she made and of every reaction she caused.

"I doubt if they'll have need of a kitchen for a very long time."

She spoke like someone who'd been there. He was more down-to-earth and practical. "Won't they get hungry?"

She never missed a beat. "Takeout works splendidly in cases like this."

He felt a little overwhelmed by the magnitude of the proposed undertaking. As well as a little overwhelmed by the woman herself.

Playing along, Bruce looked around the store. Nothing readily lent itself to this grandiose decorating scheme she was suggesting.

He turned around, half expecting her to be laughing at him for falling for her joke. She wasn't laughing. If anything, she looked serious. Maybe she really was. "And just where are you going to get all these things?"

He was going to help her, she thought. There had been a moment she'd had her doubts. "Oh, don't worry about that." She was already lifting the telephone receiver. "I have a lot of connections." Because of Elaine, she'd gotten to know a great many people who worked on the crews of various productions, as well as the head of the prop department over at Universal.

He exchanged looks with Joyce. The younger woman had an amused grin on her face, as if she was relieved that someone else was on the receiving end of Margo's enthusiasm. Obviously this kind of behavior wasn't anything new.

"Somehow, I thought you might."

Maybe he would appreciate being asked formally. She knew she had a habit of getting carried away and taking things for granted at times.

Margo paused, the receiver in her hand, her fingers hovering over the keypad. "Are you in? Or should I ask someone else to help?"

Heaven only knew what prompted him. Maybe it was because he was at a place where he was beginning to feel that he was in danger of being left behind as life galloped by. Or maybe it was because her excitement was infectious. Just like her laugh. In any case, he heard himself volunteering for God-only-knew-what in the long run.

"What, and let me miss all this fun? Count me in." He smiled wryly. "I've never been very unorthodox before."

She paused only to glance in his direction, a beatific and rather innocent smile playing on her lips as she tapped out the number of the first person on her list. "Neither have I."

The funny thing was, Bruce thought, she looked as if she actually meant it.

* * *

"And this was exactly where Lola Montenegro sat as Grant Freelancer began to ravage her." Reciting the key romantic scene from *Renegade,* Margo carefully reattached the filmy pink curtain to the corner of what had passed as a bed in the movie. "That is, he started to ravage her, but then he realized that she wasn't going to fight him off the way he anticipated. That took the pleasure away for him."

She glanced up to see Bruce, his arms crossed before his chest, watching her as if he was trying to make up his mind about something. She had no idea which side to root for, only that the way he looked at her made her feel purely female and yet strangely chaste for all that.

She continued more slowly, having just the slightest problem remembering her train of thought. "Until it occurred to him that he didn't want her the way he'd wanted all his other conquests. She was special to him. Her plan to make him back away backfired. All it did was make him want her more.

"That kiss burned up the screen around the world." Margo sighed for a moment, remembering the effect that had on her the first time she'd seen the old movie. She'd stayed up late and watched it on the old black-and-white TV, the sound down low.

And then she smiled glibly at Bruce. "Hard to imagine that they had to do it with a full complement of cast and crew looking on. It seemed so very, very private." Her eyes met his. The intensity she saw within them made her moisten lips that suddenly felt dry. "But then, that's what good acting is all about. Being able to sustain an illusion and make it seem like reality."

There was something in her voice that made him wonder if she had firsthand experience with trying to sustain illusions.

He was reading too much into it, he told himself.

"How do you remember all this?" he wanted to know. "Better yet, how do you even know all this?"

She stood back and surveyed the results of their hard work. *Perfect.*

Her years of helping Elaine on the various sets was so much a part of her, sometimes she forgot that not everyone knew that.

"I watched a great many movies when I was growing up. And what I hadn't seen, Aunt Elaine had. She loved talking about them, about her work. It was like being part of a magical world." Her expression sobered just a little as she took one last look around to make sure everything was ready. There was champagne and small finger sandwiches cooling in the refrigerator that the newlyweds could feed each other. "After being part of that other world," she said more to herself than to her patient audience, "Hollywood's make-believe was a welcome relief."

"Other world?" he asked.

Sometime, she had to remember when to disengage her mouth from her thoughts. "The one I came from." Which was as far as she intended to take that line of conversation. "Well, looks like we did it." She raised her eyes to his, an impish smile on her lips. "Do you think they'll be surprised?"

Surprised was hardly the word he'd use. "Lance is probably going to think he walked into the wrong apartment."

Margo sincerely doubted that. "Not if he married my daughter." She saw the skeptical look on his face. "I guarantee Melanie's had an effect on him. She's bound to have aroused his dormant gene," she added when he remained unconvinced.

He was having trouble following her again. "Excuse me?"

He was so adorable when he was being polite. Adorable and sexy. It made for a very potent combination. Margo took a breath.

"Imagination," she explained. "It's usually dormant

within most men. Most adults, probably. It's that part of you that can believe in anything, given enough faith.''

He glanced back at the bedroom. Straight out of *A Thousand and One Arabian Nights.* ''Your 'dormant gene' is alive and thriving, I see.''

''Always,'' she assured him. There was nothing left to do except lock up and wait for tomorrow. ''You were a dear to let me store some of their things in your garage. There's really no space at Elaine's house.''

The way she referred to the living quarters above the shop struck him as odd. ''Shouldn't you refer to that as yours by now?''

''No,'' she answered blithely. She shook her purse, listening for the telltale sound of keys. ''If anything, it belongs to Melanie.''

Was it his imagination, or did she take pride in not having a permanent place of her own? ''Do you like being a nomad?''

Margo took out the ring of keys, selecting the one for the new apartment that Melanie had left with her. Beckoning for Bruce to follow, she stepped outside the door. But as she began to place the key into the lock, Bruce took the ring from her. He locked the door himself and then returned the key ring to her.

''I think of it as an adventure.'' She slipped the keys back into her purse. ''Speaking of which, are you up for another?''

''That depends.'' He studied her for a moment. ''Will I have to lift it?''

He was a delight. ''Only a fork. I'm treating you to dinner.''

All right, he admitted it. He was old-fashioned when it came to some things, like paying when he went out with a woman. ''If you wanted to go out to dinner, Margo, all you had to do was—''

"I'm asking and I'm paying." She followed him to the carport. "I insist."

There was a tinge of embarrassment he had to bank down. Bruce turned, nearly colliding with her. "Does anyone get a chance to say no to you?"

Her smile was very confident. "Not in the last twenty-three years."

He blew out a breath. "I guess I'm too tired to set a precedent."

She never doubted it for a moment. "Good, I was counting on that."

His T-shirt adhered to his body in several areas, glued in place by sweat. He wasn't keen on the wind shifting while he was standing out here, so close to her. "I think I'd like to grab a shower first."

"Pity, I like sweaty men." He looked incredibly rugged in his worn, stonewashed jeans and faded T-shirt. "Is an hour long enough?" Margo slipped into the passenger side of his truck.

He could only shake his head. The woman was a frustrated general. "An hour will be fine."

She watched as he got in and buckled up. "Okay, you can drop me off at Elaine's. I'll be by to pick you up at—"

"I will pick you up," Bruce informed her, enunciating each word. A man had to take charge sometime.

She inclined her head, conceding. "I love a forceful man."

Yeah, right, he thought, starting the engine. But he was smiling by the time he merged into traffic.

Chapter Four

Bruce chose the restaurant. Because it was Friday night, he had his doubts about readily getting a table. But they arrived at The Moonraker at one of the few lulls the restaurant would enjoy that night. There were still a few empty tables left.

The maître d' led them to a table in the heart of the dining area. The fact that more than a few pairs of male eyes marked their passage was not lost on Bruce. Simply dressed, Margo McCloud was still a very stunning woman. Bruce had a feeling she would have made heads turn wearing sackcloth and ashes.

"We'd rather have that one." Bruce indicated an empty table with a view of the lake. It was more private, and he was suddenly feeling the need for privacy.

"Certainly."

The maître d' quickly plucked the menus he'd placed down from the table and led the way to the table Bruce requested. Helping Margo with her chair, the man appeared to linger just a moment over her. Bruce noted the appreciative glint in the man's eyes. And the envious one when he looked up at Bruce.

"I hope you will find everything satisfactory," he murmured. Moving gracefully, the maître d' changed places with a waiter who looked barely old enough to shave. The latter took their order for cocktails. A mai tai and scotch and soda.

Margo laced her fingers together before her as she looked out on the water. It was a man-made lake, but that didn't make the view any less soothing. "Do you come here often?"

There was a candle within a round, yellow-tinted bowl in the center of the table. The light flickered along her profile, slipping lovingly along the slender column of her throat like an old friend. Bruce opened the menu and forced himself to look at it, though he already knew what he was ordering.

"For business lunches and with clients when late meetings run over."

Was he deliberately being coy? No, unless she was completely mistaken, she didn't think he understood how to be coy.

"How about for pleasure? With a lady," she added since he didn't answer immediately. She saw him raise his eyebrow. That rugged, handsome face was just like a book with large print. She could read every thought. "Yes, I'm prying," she admitted without a single qualm. "I have a habit of invading other people's space, but at times, it's the only way I can find anything out. The person is usually so stunned when I ask, he tells me what I want to know without realizing that he's surrendered some of his privacy." Because she was so outgoing, she found that people forgave transgressions they would have resented in someone else. Margo took it for granted that Bruce would be no different.

There'd been a term during World War II for the way she came flying in for a sudden attack, Bruce thought.

Blitzkrieg. He maintained his silence, wondering if she would give up, having a hunch she wouldn't.

"But, since I don't spread anything I'm told around or print it on the Internet, people usually learn to relax and just talk to me." She leaned her head on her upturned palm, her eyes washing over him, giving him the impression of moving closer without actually moving a muscle. "So, talk to me. Do you? Come here for pleasure I mean."

Pleasure. It wasn't something he thought about, one way or the other. He gave it some thought now. "I did tonight."

It was like pulling teeth, Margo thought. Strong, straight white teeth that dazzled when he offered a smile. "And other than tonight?"

Bruce shrugged, setting the menu to one side, wishing the waiter would get back with his drink. "I can't remember."

She had a very strong feeling that she had just been lied to. Or at least evaded. Her amusement rose another notch. Margo moved a little further into his territory. "You don't strike me as the forgetful type."

Damn if she wasn't getting to him. Bruce had to admit she'd aroused his curiosity. "Just what type do you see me as?"

That was an easy one. She'd had him pegged from the first moment she'd laid eyes on him. "The strong, silent type."

He supposed that was as apt a description of him as any. "And does that annoy you?" Why else would she be so persistent in trying to get him to bare his soul?

"On the contrary, the strong is wonderful," her eyes flicked along his shoulders, "and silence has its place." Tongue in cheek, she proceeded to enumerate. "When you're sleeping or in the library or in a classroom during a test. But not in a conversation, because then the conversation becomes a monologue, and despite what you might think," she began, her eyes teasing him, "I really don't like hearing myself talk."

"I do," he said mildly. "Like hearing you talk," he added in case she didn't follow him. "You have a very melodious voice." He would have called it soothing if it wasn't so unnervingly sensual.

Margo cocked her head. "Even if you hear it prying into areas where it doesn't belong?"

"Even then." He cut a piece from the loaf the busboy set on their table and offered it to her. "As a matter of fact, that might have been the only thing that saved you."

Taking the slice, she shook her head. Obviously she'd missed something. "From what?"

His smile was slow, crinkling around his eyes. "From being told what you could do with your prying."

Nicely done, she thought, laughing. She sincerely doubted his virile, misplaced code of ethics allowed him to tell a woman where to get off in anything but the broadest euphemistic terms.

Bruce allowed himself a moment to savor the sound. "And there's that, too."

Her eyes narrowed as she tried to follow him. He wasn't as readable as she thought. And certainly not as ineloquent as he seemed to believe. "'That'?"

"Your laugh. If it were any sexier, it would probably come wrapped in a brown paper bag." As it was, it could make a man's imagination take flight and at the same time tighten his gut. It was the kind of laugh that understood no boundaries, took no prisoners.

Margo let out a long breath. "And still you resist telling me what I want to know."

"Have it your way." Not that he thought for one moment that she wouldn't. He'd already figured out that the woman had enormous tenacity. The kind that stemmed tides, moved mountains and eventually made even strong men capitulate. "I never come here except on business."

He was walking right into this, Margo thought, a veritable innocent. She couldn't remember when she'd enjoyed herself this immensely. "And do I come under the heading of business, or is it just that you mean business with me?"

He almost took her seriously. And then he saw the humor in her eyes. It made her look like a young girl. Which seemed only fair, seeing as how he already felt like a stuttering adolescent in her presence.

To put it in Lance's vernacular, the lady was a piece of work. "Have you thought of working for the government? They could always use someone who knows how to twist words around into verbal pretzels."

She laughed again just as the waiter arrived with their drinks. It struck Bruce that the sound of her laughter was almost like an opiate, hearing it left him wanting more—each time just a little more intently than before.

Did she laugh like that when bathed in pleasure? When she saw desire in a man's eyes as he reached for her?

He needed this drink more than he thought he did, Bruce decided, wrapping his hands around the chunky, squat glass. The small measure of amber liquid at the bottom hardly looked sufficient to counteract the effect she was having on him.

Margo curled her fingers around the stem of her glass and raised it in a toast, her eyes locking with his. "To the future."

It was, he thought, a safe enough toast. There would always be a future in the absolute sense, come what may. His had looked solid and very predictable, while hers, he was sure, was in a constant state of flux. They were, he judged, as opposite as opposites could be.

"To the future," he echoed. "And to the most beautiful woman in the room."

He had absolutely no idea he was going to say that until the words had come out. Reflecting, Bruce didn't regret saying it, he was just surprised that he had. It certainly wasn't his style, but then, the lady had a style all her own, and she seemed to coax things out of him he hadn't even guessed were there.

Like the way his mind kept drifting tonight.

Just as it had since he'd met her.

Margo paused, glass almost to her lips. She'd been complimented and toasted before, in far more flowery language than Bruce had just used. But that conservative wording had touched her. He wasn't trying to impress her, he was being sincere. She wondered if he knew how rare a trait that was.

She smiled into his eyes. "And you said you weren't good with words."

He felt out of place, as if his jacket had suddenly shrunk two sizes, pinning his arms to his sides. "Must be the restaurant," he muttered, still not sure just what had come over him. "I hold my own during business meetings here." The fact that he had worked his way up from a low level to one of the top positions in the company would have made his statement seem incredibly modest, but he saw no reason to embellish it.

He was still clinging to that business thing, Margo thought. She was beginning to believe that he actually didn't go out socially. Up until now, she'd thought Melanie was exaggerating.

Margo took a sip of her drink and let the fruity flavor slide slowly down her throat. Held his own during business meetings, did he? "One of us should dictate a letter."

Following her example, Bruce took a healthy swig of his own drink, hoping that the bitter taste would cut through the unsettled state of his nerves. He wasn't good at this sort of thing, being one on one with a woman. But he had dealt himself in for the evening and he was determined to see it through. Besides, there were worse things than sitting across from a beautiful woman as twilight settled in.

He raised his glass to her. "One of us already knows how to dictate."

She twirled the stem slowly between her thumb and fore-finger, her eyes never left his. "You think I'm pushy." It wasn't a question. Margo already knew what he thought. It was right there in his eyes.

Pushy sounded too much like an insult. Diplomatically he tempered the description. "I think that you always get your way."

Was he just being polite? Did her behavior irritate him? She wasn't sure. The writing in the large print book had suddenly become small and illegible. "Is that such a bad thing? Most people want their own way." She ran the tip of her tongue along her lips, savoring the taste of her drink. "And I'm harmless enough."

It took effort to draw his eyes away from her mouth and the slight damp sheen there. And more effort to draw his mind away from the thoughts that were springing up because of it.

"I doubt that you were ever considered harmless, Margo. Not even five minutes after you were born." When he raised his eyes to hers, he saw that they had clouded. "Did I say something wrong?"

She shook her head. "No."

But he had, Bruce thought. He'd somehow unwittingly stumbled onto something that upset her. For one fleeting instant, something he'd said had struck a wound, an old scar, making it bleed again.

At a loss, wishing he had some of the verbal skills that came so easily to Margo, Bruce reached for his menu. In an effort to smooth things over, he changed the conversation to something banal.

He pretended to peruse the main-course items embossed in dark script on the menu. "See anything here you like?"

"Yes."

When he raised his eyes to ask her what, he saw that she

was looking at him. The smile on her lips was enigmatic. Nevertheless, he felt his pulse speed up just a shade over what the medical profession agreed was acceptable.

Maybe it was a good thing his tongue had gotten too large for his mouth. Otherwise, he would have swallowed it.

Bruce reached for his water glass and took a long sip. His throat was parched. He couldn't remember when he'd done so much talking, not even when he'd chaired the meeting that brought about the eventual merger of Phillips Inc. with his own Weston Data Corp., forming Weston Phillips. From the salad to the main course and then dessert, Margo had plied him with question after question, looking so taken, so absorbed by his answers that he had just kept on talking.

Like that damn windup toy that ran on eternal batteries. Him, who'd hardly strung together ten words a day that didn't have to do with his job.

She would have made an excellent interrogator, he decided, placing his glass back on the table. She drew information out of him as if she were merely turning on a tap. Over the course of the past hour, he'd heard himself telling her all about Ellen, about their life together until hers had abruptly been cut short. Comforted by the surprising depth of Margo's sympathy, he'd gone on to confide about the pain he'd gone through, living without someone he'd been certain he was destined to grow old with.

And he'd made no effort to absolve himself of blame when he told her how the schism between Lance and him had come about. He'd never blamed Lance for any of that.

"But, Lance," she observed tactfully, making swirls in the remainder of the whipped cream on her plate with her fork, "was to blame for perpetuating it after you tried to apologize and make amends."

Over the years he'd had ample opportunity to examine

the situation from Lance's point of view. "Under the circumstances, you can see why he didn't choose to run back to me with open arms just because I wanted to pretend it never happened." Problems didn't go away because you denied their existence, they went away because you faced them. "Just because *I* wanted to pretend that I hadn't disappeared from his life and left him to be raised by Bess for an entire decade, didn't mean *he* did."

He'd lost himself in his work after Ellen had died, work that had absolutely no meaning for him anymore, except that it allowed him to send regular checks for his son's keep and somehow pay his sister back for taking on the responsibility he couldn't bring himself to shoulder.

Margo sighed over what had been, just a few minutes ago, a plate with a thin slice of Boston cream pie on it. She could have eaten six and asked for more, only to watch them all adhere themselves directly to her hips. It was safer to concentrate on what Bruce was saying to her.

"You wouldn't have been in the running for Father of the Year," she conceded, "but since you made the effort to apologize, you could be forgiven your reaction. It only happened because you loved too much, cared too much. Sometimes," Margo added gently, "that throws you off kilter."

She seemed so clearly in possession of herself, he couldn't help but wonder out loud, "Have you ever loved too much?"

"Every time," she laughed lightly. Bringing the fork to her lips, she removed the last bit of whipped cream on it by touching her tongue to the tip of the prongs. Bruce would have sworn he'd never seen anything more sensual in his life.

"I mean really," he insisted, not completely sure why getting an answer was so important to him. Maybe he was just paying her back for drawing him out the way she had. Or maybe he was trying to ignore the fact that watching her was creating a very unsettling sensation within him. "After all, you grilled me, the least you can do is answer a few of my questions."

She'd be the first to admit that it was only fair. "I'll answer any question you ask."

She was being evasive, he thought. She did that well. "I already asked one."

"So you did." She set her fork down and began, perhaps a little too breezily. "All right, I probably did love Melanie's father too much. At least enough to cloud my judgment. I actually thought he'd be happy about the baby. I should have realized that no eighteen-year-old boy in his right mind was going to be happy about becoming a father."

He took exception. "I was." Once the news had settled in, once he'd had time to become accustomed to the idea, he'd been overjoyed. The baby was physical evidence of the love he bore for Ellen.

Margo believed him. That made him one in a million. But he hadn't been her one, so it didn't count.

"You are a very rare individual, Bruce. There aren't many men like you. Believe me, I know." She touched his hand as she spoke, giving it a confidential squeeze. "As I told you at the reception, your wife was a very lucky woman."

Bruce had always thought of himself as the lucky one, not Ellen. She'd had to put up with his faults, with a lifestyle that had been far below the one she'd been raised in. Her parents, appalled by what she'd done and her subsequent refusal to have an abortion, had disowned her. They were married with exactly thirty dollars between them. It was Bess who had come to their rescue, giving them a place to stay until they got on their feet. It took him a long time to work his way up to where he could afford to give Ellen the things she'd deserved.

And that had lasted all too short a time.

The waiter arrived with the check, saving Bruce from having to answer Margo's comment. Bruce silently blessed him.

The man discreetly placed the small tray beside Bruce's elbow. Margo reached for it, but she was too slow. Bruce was already taking out his charge card. He placed it over the bill.

Margo withdrew her hand, pinning him with a reproving look. "I thought we agreed that I was going to pay for dinner."

"You agreed, and voted for me," he pointed out. "Besides," he handed the tray over to the waiter, "possession is nine-tenths of the law, and the tray with the check was on my side of the table."

She should have realized that he wasn't about to let her pay. He was too old-fashioned to allow that. Though she considered herself the epitome of a liberated woman and had for a long time, she had to admit that it was rather nice to be treated as if she belonged on a pedestal. At least for a little while.

"I'm beginning to think that you don't always play as fair as I thought you did."

"I play fair, Margo," he said honestly, "but I play by my rules. One of the prime rules is that you always pay for the lady." He expected more of a debate, something along the lines of this being the nineties and his being a dinosaur. Instead, she merely shook her head. "What's the matter?"

She didn't think men like Bruce existed, except in caves. She certainly hadn't expected to think that old-fashioned was charming. Margo was surprised on both counts. "I just can't understand why some woman hasn't snapped you up and placed you on her mantelpiece."

Bruce hardly thought of himself as a trophy. "Possibly because I'm a lot heavier than I look." The waiter returned, silently offering him a pen and a charge slip to use it on.

He had a bold hand, Margo thought, observing the way

Bruce wrote his signature. The sign of a man who was in charge and comfortable with himself.

"Chivalrous with a sense of humor, you're almost too good to be true."

He certainly wasn't going to comment on that. Tucking the slip around his card, he pocketed both as the waiter withdrew, smiling broadly at the tip he'd just gotten. "Ready to go?"

Margo reached for her purse. "I was born ready."

He didn't doubt it for a moment.

"Would you like to come up for a nightcap?" Margo lingered at her door, reluctant to call an end to the evening. It had been one of the most enjoyable ones she'd had in a very long time.

He was tempted, but he shook his head. "I'd better not. The police in Bedford run a very strict show. I'd rather not have to spend the night in one of their jail cells."

She didn't push it. She'd done enough pushing for one night, she thought. Still, part of her was fascinated by a man who hadn't put any moves on her the entire evening. Technically, this counted as their second date no matter which way she looked at it. There had been the wedding reception, and they had just spent the entire afternoon together, rearranging Melanie and Lance's apartment. And in all that time, he'd been nothing but polite.

It was sweet, but at the same time it did make her wonder if she was slipping.

Wasn't he interested?

"I'd bail you out," she promised.

He was serious, although one more drink, especially if it was wine or beer, would hardly qualify him as drunk. He'd only had the one drink at the beginning of dinner.

If anything, Margo had been far more intoxicating than the alcohol in his glass.

"There'd be no bail set until morning. An overnight stay

is mandatory.'' He had a few friends on the force and knew the rules. "Like I said, they take a very dim view of driving under the influence. At least alcoholic influence,'' he amended, unable to draw his eyes away from her. From the way the moonlight was reverently touching her skin. With or without that nightcap, he was going to be guilty of driving under the influence when he went home. "Well, good night, Margo, I had a very nice time."

He couldn't seem to get his feet to move, to create distance between them.

"Yeah, me, too." She looked up at him, wishing he would kiss her. It seemed strangely ironic. She thought nothing of kissing people, of pressing her lips fleetingly or passionately against another pair, whether in fun or in earnest. But this time she wanted the first move to be his.

So that it counted.

Margo couldn't remember when she'd been this silly. Or when she'd wanted to be kissed so much.

Bruce was still standing there, unable to force himself to walk away. It was almost as if something else, something that was very much out of practice, insisted on taking over. The distant ache that had been slowly evolving ever since dinner felt vaguely familiar.

"Help me out here," he said quietly.

"If I can." She should have remained amused. Why she suddenly felt nervous was beyond her.

But she did.

He touched her cheek with the tips of his fingers and watched in fascination as her eyes fluttered ever so slightly in response. "I don't remember. Is this the part where the boy kisses the girl just before he leaves?"

"This is the part." Her voice sounded oddly disembodied to her own ear.

"Good," he replied softly, "that means I didn't forget how it's done."

Cupping the back of her head with his hand, Bruce softly

brought his mouth down to hers. He told himself that he'd had no intention of kissing her when he brought her to her door. He'd only wanted to make sure she was safe.

It was he who wasn't safe. He found himself a prisoner of the very action he initiated.

No, it couldn't be called action, it was impulse that had led him to this. Impulse, that wild, fleeting thing that urged a man to do things he shouldn't. Things that were dangerous. Like skydiving with an untested chute, or hang gliding.

Or kissing Margo.

He probably would have been better prepared for the first two than the last. She took his breath away from the very first second his lips touched hers.

Until now, he'd considered himself a normal male who'd had a genuinely satisfying relationship with a woman he had sincerely loved. That meant that there were very few surprises left on the male-female front. Or so he'd thought.

He was wrong. Very wrong.

A rush went through him and he could only go with it, traveling to wherever it deigned to take him. Reflexively deepening the kiss, it was a struggle to keep himself grounded, to keep the world from spinning away.

They were right, Margo realized. Those people who claimed that Still Waters Run Deep, they were right. Bruce might have been quiet by nature, but in no way was quiet equated with dull. Not in this case. She'd sensed his sexiness, but she'd never sensed the quiet power, the delicious taste of the man.

Margo's hands curled along the hard muscles of his biceps as she let herself be drawn into the center of the kiss. She was surprised by the force, by the passion of her own response. Surprised and delighted.

This was better than any movie she'd ever watched, any vicarious experience she'd ever conjured up. This was like running into a storm and being swept up in its embrace, in its power.

And then, abruptly, the storm ended. Just like that. Bruce drew away from her, leaving her dazed and wanting more.

She was careful not to exhale too loudly, afraid he'd detect just how shaky she felt right now.

Oh, boy. She felt as if she was perilously close to being knocked off her feet.

"You didn't," she murmured, surprised that she could still form words and get them out of her mouth.

He felt shell-shocked. And something more than that. Something he didn't like feeling. "Didn't what?"

Was something wrong? He sounded so stiff, so formal. "Forget how it was done." She studied his face. There *was* something wrong. "It's done just this way," she continued quietly, afraid of making him disappear if she raised her voice. "Except not always quite this good."

He made no comment, no effort to sustain what had just happened or follow it to its logical conclusion. Another man would have asked for that nightcap now, and taken her, once they were upstairs. Instead, Bruce looked at her like a man who'd just realized he was standing in a patch of poison ivy.

"Good night, Margo." And with that Bruce left. Quickly.

Chapter Five

Bruce supposed, as he turned his car down Main Street the next afternoon, that some men would have called him crazy, or at the very least, inordinately stupid. His best friend, Paul Giordano, would have probably volunteered to drive him to the nearest shrink.

From the outside, he had to admit that it must have made for an incredible scenario. There he'd been with a beautiful, vibrant and seemingly willing woman, and rather than see where the evening could go, all he could think to do was backpedal as fast as he was able and get the hell out of there.

His father, had he still been alive, would have been vastly disappointed in him. But then, his father had never believed in or understood what it meant to have a lasting love. The truth of it was, Bruce didn't want to find out where the evening could have gone. Because he really didn't want to go there. Not if he examined his heart in the cold, sober light of day, and that was what ultimately counted.

He'd loved one woman his entire adult life, and he figured that qualified him as one of the lucky ones. He wasn't out for another relationship which, for him, was the only real reason to be on intimate terms with a woman.

But he *was* out, he thought, ambiguous feelings once more taking residence within him. Out among the living, to quote Bess on the subject, a subject she dearly loved harping on lately. His sister had turned up her volume now that he and Lance were finally reconciled.

The woman desperately needed a hobby.

And as for him, he needed to hurry up or he was going to be late. He was going to the airport to pick up Melanie and Lance. When he'd arrived home last night, there'd been a message on his answering machine from Lance, asking him if he could be there.

He smiled to himself. It felt nice, being asked for a favor by his son. There was absolutely nothing about this newly restored relationship that he intended to take for granted.

Checking to his left, he shifted lanes. Their plane landed at two. Following Murphy's Law, planes were only late if you weren't. If he arrived late, the plane would undoubtedly land on time, if not early.

Bruce pressed down on the accelerator, just squeaking through a light that was about to turn red.

He figured that his son and new daughter-in-law would be tired after their long flight from Hawaii. There'd been a forty-five-minute layover at LAX before they boarded a plane that would bring them to John Wayne Airport in Orange County. The last thing they needed was to stand around a crowded airport, waiting for him to show up.

Taking advantage of an opening, Bruce changed lanes again, then jockeyed for position until he managed to get all the way over to the left. Traffic was heavy this time of day but he finally reached the no-man's-land known as the airport parking lot and then sprinted toward the U.S. Airlines terminal that was three parking lots away.

At least his early mornings at the gym weren't wasted,

he thought, weaving his way past a slow-moving group of five.

When he made it past the terminal's electronic doors, he paused to catch his breath and glance at his watch. Five minutes to spare. Congratulating himself, Bruce took time for two deep, cleansing breaths before he walked toward the nearest arrival-departure board.

Looking up, he searched for Lance and Melanie's flight number.

"The plane's landing at Gate Five," the smoky voice to his left informed him.

Like a film in slow motion, Bruce turned around. Somehow he'd manage to walk right by Margo without even seeing her.

He was probably the only man in the terminal who hadn't. She was wearing light blue shorts, the edges just brushing the tops of her thighs, a navy halter and three-inch high white mules. Typical sunny California attire. She looked, for all the world, like a woman who had several years to go before she reached her thirtieth birthday.

Bruce had to remind himself to breathe.

Last night flashed vividly across his brain like lights during a power surge. Last night, when he'd behaved like nothing short of a jackass. He had absolutely no idea what to say to her, how to begin to explain why he had left her so abruptly.

He didn't know whether to be relieved, mystified or wary, because Margo acted as if nothing had happened.

"I wasn't sure if you were supposed to be picking them up." She appeared pleased to see him there. "So I thought it wouldn't hurt to play it safe and show up, just in case."

She glanced toward the rear of the terminal, but there was no activity at Gate Five, except for a flight attendant who was unlocking the double doors.

He was acquainted with that, with playing it safe. It was the only way he knew how to play. Gingerly Bruce picked up the thread of conversation Margo had extended to him. "Lance asked me if I would. Pick them up, I mean."

She nodded. He was avoiding her eyes. Probably would feel better if he could avoid her altogether, she thought. Well, it wasn't going to happen. Not until a few things were set right.

Margo had slipped her hands into her pockets, making the material around her hips strain as it hugged each curve that much closer. Bruce drew in another cleansing breath. He figured his heart could use the oxygen.

"Well, I'll just stick around, anyway." She paused, letting that sink in, then moved in for the main event. Running into him like this spared her the trouble of making a phone call. "I thought it might be nice if I made them an early dinner, so they wouldn't have to bother going to a restaurant to eat." The champagne and finger sandwiches she'd left in their refrigerator were for later tonight. "That way they don't have to worry about food until, oh, Thursday or Friday." She smiled, thinking how nice it might be, living on love and little else. "I made enough for a small army. You're welcome to come, too, if you'd like."

His first reaction was to turn her down. But there was something at war with his choice right from the start.

"No, I—you cook?" He couldn't imagine her in the kitchen. In the bathroom he could, taking a bubble bath; in the bedroom, wearing a smile and little else; even in the boardroom, slaughtering the opposition; but not the kitchen. That was far too mundane a place for someone like Margo.

Her shoulders, as smooth and creamy as the center of the candy bar that was his weakness, straightened as she informed him proudly, "Damn straight I do." And then that same sexy smile, the one that had nearly undone him last night, slipped over her lips. "I'm a woman of many talents."

Of that he had absolutely no doubt. "On second thought, yes, I'd like to come."

As far as he could ascertain, she seemed perfectly willing to let last night's behavior slip quietly into the land of past, inexplicable deeds. Bruce debated following her lead. Gratefully. At least she wasn't one of those women who picked apart and explored every action, every word, from all sides. His best friend's ex-wife had been one of those. She'd almost sent Paul over the edge before he'd finally called it a day.

But because Margo made no reference to the way he'd left her last night, he found himself thinking that she deserved an explanation. He just wasn't certain he could give her one, at least not a coherent one.

Still, he had to try. He figured he owed it to her. "I—Margo—about last night." This was going even worse than he'd anticipated. Bruce tried again. "I didn't mean to…"

"Bolt and run like a rabbit in hunting season?" she supplied pleasantly when his pause threatened to trail off indefinitely.

"A rabbit?" His dark brows drew together in a frown. "Is that what I looked like?"

"You didn't look like a rabbit," she conceded graciously. Her eyes washed over his torso. If the man had an ounce of fat on him, he was carrying it around in his pockets. "Not unless rabbits are suddenly working out. But you did bolt like one." Her smile was as warm as it was amused. "I had no intention of skinning you and using your pelt as a trophy."

Without meaning to, she'd made him feel like an even bigger fool. But there had been a very valid reason for his abrupt departure last night. At least, it had seemed valid at the time. Now he was having difficulty finding the words.

"I didn't mean to leave like that. It's just that—that—"

Seeing the look on his face, she read between the lines. It wasn't difficult. Languages might have been her vocation, but studying people was her hobby.

"You felt guilty kissing someone who wasn't your wife?"

It was more than that. The kissing part didn't matter, although it had knocked his shoes off and curled his socks. It was the feeling behind it that had mattered, that had startled him into retreat.

He had felt something when he kissed Margo. Felt a desire that he hadn't experienced since Ellen died. A desire that was so large it had almost overwhelmed him. He'd wanted, in that one passionate instance, to take Margo to bed. To make love with her and enjoy her.

That was what he was feeling guilty about. About being disloyal.

About being alive while Ellen wasn't.

But it was all much too complicated to begin to explain. After all, they barely knew one another.

So he took the easy way out and nodded. "I guess that was it in a nutshell."

There was more to it, Margo thought, looking into his eyes. But everyone needed their privacy. She was the first to know that.

"You weren't cheating on your wife, Bruce," she said gently. She laid her hand on his arm, creating an intimate, impervious force field around them. Though there was the roar of planes overhead and noise all around them, he heard only her. "You weren't cheating at all, except maybe on yourself. It's okay to feel again. If Ellen was half the person you led me to believe she was, she wouldn't have wanted you to bury yourself. She would have wanted you to be happy."

"I am happy," he insisted. The response was automatic. He'd uttered it often enough when Bess got on his case. "Relatively happy," he amended when she continued to look at him with her wide, luminous blue eyes. Eyes that weren't about to allow him to get away with a half-truth.

Margo knew when to back away. She'd said what she

had to say about the matter. The rest would take care of itself. Life always did.

"All right," she said brightly, "then you'll come for dinner? It's at Elaine's. I thought we'd take them over there first, then go to their apartment after they've had dinner." She was saving the apartment for dessert, she thought, looking forward to seeing Lance's reaction to her handiwork. Their handiwork, she amended, remembering the good-natured way Bruce had put up with being ordered around the entire afternoon.

"I'll come to dinner," Bruce agreed. The way he saw it, he really had no choice. He couldn't very well not be there for Melanie and Lance's first official meal back. Not after it had taken so long to mend relations between his son and him. Besides, he had to admit he was a little curious about Margo's so-called culinary abilities. He was still skeptical that she could do anything beyond zapping prepackaged meals in a microwave.

A movement in the rear of the terminal caught his eye. Looking over Margo's head, he saw the first of the disembarking passengers trickling through the gate. "I think their plane just landed."

As she turned around to look, Margo linked her arm with his in one fluid motion. "Let's go." She gave his arm a gentle tug, drawing him toward the gate as the number of people in the general area multiplied.

Searching through the crowd for either familiar face, Bruce was vaguely aware of the satisfying sensation generated by having her arm joined with his.

Just as he predicted, Bruce saw Lance's jaw slacken and drop the moment he walked through the door of his apartment later that evening.

Stunned, Lance stared at the re-creation of the throne room from *Knights of the Round Table*. His expression was reminiscent of Dorothy's the first time she laid eyes on the munchkins in Oz, Bruce thought.

It took Lance almost a full minute to recover his voice. When he did, he turned to look at his father. "What the hell happened?"

Margo moved between the two men. Taking Lance's hand, she drew him into the room, a mother coaxing her child into the barber's chair for the first time.

"I took a few liberties." She studied his face, waiting for shock to give way to pleasure. It was already there in her daughter's expression. But then, Melanie had grown up around this kind of thing. "Don't worry, all your things are safely stored at your father's house. This all has to go back by the end of next week."

"Next week?" Lance echoed. How was he supposed to live with this for the next six days?

Like a man trapped in a dream he wasn't fully convinced was not a nightmare, Lance walked toward the bedroom. He stopped dead in the doorway. The bedroom was even more incredible than the living room.

The sharp, pleased squeal behind him told Lance that Melanie, at least, was thrilled with what she saw. He supposed, given her background, he could see why she would be.

But there had been very little make-believe in his background. He wasn't sure he could handle this.

Lance looked from his father to Margo. That his feet-firmly-planted-on-the-ground father had taken part in this surprised him almost as much as the decorating job did.

"What are we supposed to do with all this for a week?" he wanted to know.

Melanie smiled up at him before either Margo or Bruce could answer. She ran her hand along the circular bed, which was basically one huge, round pillow that took up half the room. Filmy curtains hung from the ceiling, swaying seductively in the breeze coming from the window. It reinforced the seductive look in her eyes. "Oh, a few things come to mind."

Very slowly, like a flower unfolding its petals in the morning sun, the various scenarios came to him. Lance grinned, slipping his arm around his wife's waist, pulling her toward him. "Yeah, I guess I can think of a few."

Good for you, Lance, thought Margo. *Melanie made the right choice after all.*

Her last doubt about him laid to rest, Margo began to edge away. It was time for her work to be savored, up close and personal.

"We'll just leave you to explore those possibilities." She slanted an expectant look toward Bruce, waiting for him to take the hint.

Belatedly, Melanie looked at her mother. "Oh, but you don't have to leave yet."

Margo laughed. The protest lacked the right note of enthusiasm. "I love you for lying." Cupping her chin in her hand, Margo kissed her daughter's cheek. "But, yeah, we do."

Coming up behind Melanie, Lance slipped his arms around her shoulders, holding her to him. The magnitude of his happiness amazed him. Just being happy at all was still very new to him.

"Thanks, both of you." He looked at his father. "You've been great."

"And we'll be greater once we're gone." Margo winked at him. Taking Bruce's hand in hers, she urged him through the door.

"It was a great dinner, Mom," Lance raised his voice, calling after her.

"Anytime I'm in town," she promised. Margo closed the door behind her. She grinned at Bruce as they walked toward his car.

It *had* been a great dinner, Bruce thought. A three-course dinner good enough to have been served at a five-star res-

taurant. She'd really surprised him. But then, he was beginning to realize that Margo McCloud was actually one
big continuous surprise.

As he stopped at his car, he noticed the wide grin on her
face. She looked like a teenager bursting with a secret.
"What?"

She glanced over her shoulder at the ground-floor apartment they'd just left. "I bet he's got her clothes off already."

The brash prediction stunned Bruce. And then he
laughed, shaking his head. "Tell me, are you always this
direct?" He unlocked the passenger side and opened the
door for her.

"Usually." Margo got in and closed the door, turning
toward him as he slid in behind the steering wheel. "Besides, why shouldn't they enjoy each other? They're married, they're young and they're in love." She sighed. It
sounded like a script from an old romantic comedy. "For
them, life is perfect."

Melanie was everything he ever could have wished for,
for his son. He knew Lance would be good to her. Watching them over dinner tonight, he'd seen firsthand just how
good they were for each other. His son was a changed man.
Less hard, less guarded, more open to laughter. He thought
of the redecorating job he'd taken part in yesterday. Maybe
fantasy did have a strong toehold in this world, at that.

"I hope it always stays that way."

Amen to that, she thought.

"I'd toast that wish," Margo told him, "but I seem to
be without a drink in my hand."

Pulling his seat belt around him, Bruce stopped short of
slipping the metal tongue into the slot on the side of his
seat. He looked at her, not quite sure if he was picking up
a signal or not. It had been years since he'd thought of
picking up any signals at all.

"Is that a hint?"

"No, that was an observation." She paused, wondering. Was that his way of asking her out? "Why, would you like to go somewhere for a drink?"

Maybe it was better if he left well enough alone. Still, he didn't want to be rude. She'd gone out of her way to be nice to him as well as his son. And he had to admit, he really did like her company, even if it did unsettle him at times.

"No, not unless you do."

They could go around and around like this all night, she thought.

"They did this scene in *Marty,*" she told him, "and it played much better with Ernest Borgnine in the lead." Her eyes narrowed as she looked at Bruce more closely. Maybe things would go better for them if she was blunt about the situation. "Do I make you uncomfortable, Bruce?"

He thought of lying, but figured she'd see right through it. "Yes." It wasn't so much that she made him uncomfortable, he reasoned, as he was uncomfortable with the feelings she brought to the foreground within him.

Well, he was honest; Margo would give him that. But so was she. "I'm sorry to hear that, because I've been trying my damnedest to put you at your ease." She'd already decided that they would be friends. If anything else came of their association, that would just reinforce that friendship. She wouldn't have it any other way. Lance and Melanie's happiness was very important to her and he was an integral part of that. She was determined to bring him out.

"Provided this marriage lasts," she continued, "and from what I've observed, it gives every indication of doing just that, you and I are going to be running into one another off and on over the course of the next forty years. I'd hate to think that you'd be dreading the encounter, thinking of me as an ordeal you have to face, like a trip to the dentist."

Maybe he shouldn't have admitted that he was uncomfortable in her presence. After all, he was confident his discomfort would fade once he became used to her. In about a decade or so.

"I don't think of you like a trip to the dentist, Margo—"

Margo grinned. "Keep going, I'm a sucker for flattery."

She made him laugh. Some of the tension left his body and he felt himself beginning to relax again. "I shouldn't have said you make me uncomfortable. The truth is, I make me uncomfortable."

"You are going to explain that, aren't you?" she prodded.

He was. To both their satisfaction, he hoped. Cautiously Bruce felt his way around in this unexplored region that he suddenly found himself in. "It's just that I never expected to even look at another woman."

By looking, she knew he meant taking an interest in. The unintentional admission made something stir within her. She told herself that the little thrill she felt was only because she felt physically attracted to him. What woman wouldn't be?

There was a tiny spider trying to make its way across the dashboard. Margo leaned forward and cupped her hand around it, then gently deposited it outside the car. When she looked back at Bruce, she saw he'd been watching her, bemused.

"No one was ever convicted for just looking," she said.

Another woman would have squashed the spider, or asked him to. He liked the fact that she was compassionate, even toward something so insignificant as a tiny spider. His eyes held hers. "We did more than look last night."

Some would have called what happened last night next to nothing, Margo knew. But they hadn't been on the receiving end of his kiss, and she had. She had to admit it had unnerved her a little.

How much more had it unnerved a man who'd thought he'd permanently buried his heart along with his wife?

"Yes, we did." A tension rippled through her just then.

She rolled down the window on her side. There wasn't enough air in the car. Keeping her voice light, she downplayed the incident. "We enjoyed each other's company. That isn't a crime, either, especially since we are both single adults." She'd almost added consenting, but that wouldn't have been entirely accurate just yet. He wasn't altogether consenting, which, in a way, made the situation much more exciting to her.

She made it sound so reasonable. He supposed that to someone else it was. "I must sound like a fool to you."

Margo was quick to vehemently deny that, because he was anything but a fool. "No, you don't. You sound like a warm, sensitive man, and I sincerely pray that your genes are alive and well in Lance because then I *know* my daughter is going to have a wonderful life ahead of her."

She blew out a breath. Very close to her door, one determined cricket was sending out a signal for a mate. That wasn't Bruce's problem, she thought wryly.

"As for the rest of it, if you're worried about entanglements, don't. I'm only here temporarily." The streetlight almost directly behind them illuminated the inside of the car and she could see the way his brow furrowed quizzically. "The firm that sent me to Greece closed their foreign office, which means that at the moment, I'm out of a job. But another one will come up soon and I'll be off again, teaching some other group of lost American souls the language of the country they're working in," she added quickly, in case he thought she was down on her luck. "There's a great calling for what I do. Until then, why don't we just let things go along at their own pace?"

Up to a few minutes ago, that was exactly what he'd been afraid of. But now he wasn't exactly sure. "Sounds good to me."

No more than to her. With that settled and out of the way, Margo glanced at her watch, angling it to make out the face. They'd been sitting there almost ten minutes.

"Fine, now I suggest that we either start the engine or start necking, because this is the longest I've ever sat in a parked car without one of those two things happening."

He'd been holding on to the key the entire time. As he put it into the ignition, he heard her snap her fingers. "Damn, I had a feeling you were going to do that."

He looked at her, then jerked a thumb at two older women who were very obviously watching them from their window just to the left of the carport. "If I neck with you, it damn well isn't going to be in front of an audience."

Margo only sighed. "You would never have made a very good actor with that kind of an attitude, Bruce."

He made a noise that sounded suspiciously like a grunt. "I guess I'll just have to give back my Screen Actors Guild union card."

Maybe she was beginning to rub off on him, just a little. She couldn't have explained exactly why that pleased her as much as it did, she only enjoyed the feeling. "I guess so."

The sound of her laughter wafted through the still night air as he pulled out of the carport and turned down the street to drive her home. It made for good company.

Chapter Six

"Bruce, old buddy, how good's your Italian these days?"

Bruce looked up from the progress report on his desk to Paul Giordano. The project had been his baby once, but was now in the hands of a design and development team. Fifteen people tweaking and fine-tuning a program that once would have taken Paul and him a month of burning the midnight oil to complete. He missed being able to be in on the hands-on stage. Peering over someone else's shoulder to get a glimpse of what was going on just wasn't the same thing, he thought. The money had been less in those days, but the rewards, the intrinsic ones, had been far greater than what he experienced now.

With a sigh he closed the report, giving his best friend his attention. As much attention as he could give anyone these days. Lately it seemed as if he was perpetually preoccupied. And he didn't want to be.

Italian. What had brought this on? "As good as it's always been. I can say hello and goodbye and, thanks to a movie with Gina Lollobrigida I saw as a kid, I can also say good evening." He studied Paul's thin face. He knew something was up. "Why?"

Though they were both in the loop, only Paul paid attention to what was going on. Bruce, he'd noted out loud more than once, seemed satisfied getting information third-hand. He wasn't into office gossip. Except this time the gossip concerned him directly.

Pleased to be the one to tell him, Paul doled the information out slowly, seeing how long it would take to get Bruce really interested. "You're going to need a lot more than that."

Bruce arched a brow. Paul was into games. Since he liked Paul a great deal, he tolerated the games. "I repeat—why?"

Five inches shorter and somewhat slighter than Bruce, Paul plopped himself on top of his friend's desk, making himself comfortable. "Because otherwise your associations are going to be very limited, and you'll starve to death inside two weeks."

Bruce pinned him with a look that wasn't altogether the font of unending patience it usually was. He found himself growing edgy these days, something that was completely out of character for him. He strove to keep his voice even. "I've got a meeting with Jessop in half an hour about a new program they're working on. Am I going to have to beat this out of you?"

Thoroughly enjoying himself, Paul decided to surrender the news. "All right, all right." Small brown eyes keenly watched Bruce's face as he spoke. "Word's come down that the powers that be, meaning Weston," Paul said in a totally unnecessary aside, Tom Weston being the VP in charge of their division, "have chosen the location for our first international conquest, and guess who's going to lead the charge?"

He hadn't even seen this coming. Bruce rocked back in

his chair, stunned by the information. "They're sending me to Italy?"

"That's the plan. If certain details get ironed out, you're the man the company wants to head the office in Florence, Italy." Unable to remain anyplace for long, Paul hopped off the desk and began to prowl around the office he spent more time inhabiting than his own. "Man, I envy you. All those beautiful Italian women…"

As his voice trailed off, Paul scrutinized the man who'd been his best friend for the past twelve years. A trace of wistfulness slipped in, just as it always did. If he were that tall and that good-looking, what he could do….

"On second thought, it'd probably be wasted on a guy like you." Paul shook his head mournfully. You'd think, after a twelve-year association, he would have rubbed off on the guy, at least a little. "You wouldn't notice a beautiful woman if you tripped over her and she had her foot on your Adam's apple."

Bruce laughed at the ludicrous image. "Oh, I think I'd notice then."

Paul was unconvinced as he shoved his fisted hands into his pockets. "I wouldn't take any bets on it. You have got to be the most self-contained man I've ever met." The very thought of Bruce's life-style depressed the hell out of him. Bruce was as celibate as a monk. Probably more. "Don't you sometimes just want to—you know, be with a woman?"

It seemed that everywhere Bruce turned, he was hearing the same song and dance. Bess wanted him socializing and Paul wanted him racking up conquests from one end of Orange County to the other. Why wasn't anyone happy just to leave him as he was? And why did he feel so damn restless lately, like he was no longer sure just where he did belong?

"I'm with women all the time, Paul," he pointed out mildly. The company employed a host of women, from management on down. He interacted with them frequently for hundreds of reasons.

Paul sighed, exasperated. Bruce knew what he meant. "A naked woman."

"No, don't run into many of those," Bruce agreed after giving the matter some thought. Humor touched his eyes as he looked at Paul. "I think there's a law against running around like that, isn't there?"

Maybe it was the thought of being passed over for the Florence office. Or maybe, more on target, it was that he was going to miss Bruce once his friend was gone. Whatever the case, Paul found himself residing just this side of irritable. "I worry about you." He leaned over the desk, his hands splayed out, his face low, meeting Bruce's. "A guy with your looks, it's just not natural. Every man needs a little female companionship once in a while." He could see he wasn't getting through. "Hell, even camels have to refuel once in a while. You know, you keep all that pent up, one day there's going to be a major explosion." Paul paused dramatically, letting his prediction sink in. "First Mount Saint Helens, then you."

Bruce wrote his initials beside his name on the report's cover sheet and placed it in his out-box. "When it's about to happen, I'll give you enough time to alert the news media."

The man wasn't getting the point. "Bruce—"

Because he detected a genuine note of concern, Bruce turned in his chair and looked at his friend. "Would it make you feel better if I told you I went out with a woman just last week?"

Paul rolled his eyes. "Bess." It wasn't a guess. Bruce was always taking Bess out to a restaurant or to a concert. He couldn't think of anything more depressing than having to go out with your own sister if you wanted female companionship.

Margo's wide mouth, curved in a sensual smile, streaked

across his mind like a fire engine called to a five-alarm blaze. "No, it wasn't Bess."

"Who, then?" Suspicion warred with curiosity across Paul's face.

Bruce looked at the other man, knowing exactly how this was going to go over at first mention. "My son's mother-in-law."

The expression on Paul's face was by turns incredulous, then disgusted. "Oh, terrific, some geriatric woman with corns and an overbearing attitude." He blew out a breath that was pure frustration, as if he was out of ways to get to Bruce. "That's not what I meant."

Instead of saying anything in his defense, Bruce reached into his inside pocket and took out the photograph Lance had given him the other day, showing him dancing with Margo at the reception. Lance had passed it on, along with a comment that they looked good together. Bruce wasn't sure why he hadn't taken it out of his breast pocket when he'd arrived home, but now he was glad he hadn't. Without saying a word in either his or Margo's defense, he merely held up the photograph for Paul's perusal.

Paul blinked, then covered his heart with his hand, as if he meant to keep it from leaping out. Impressed, he took the photograph from Bruce and studied it.

"Now *that's* what I mean by a woman." Several shades of disbelief had passed over his face when he looked up to stare at Bruce. "*That's* Lance's mother-in-law?"

Plucking a tissue from the dispenser on the side of his desk, Bruce offered it to Paul in trade. "If you're through drooling…" He reclaimed the photograph. Though he told himself its only value was that it had been taken at his son's reception, he still tucked it gently back into his pocket.

Paul slumped against the edge of his desk, pretending to be in shock. "Why didn't they make mothers-in-law like that when I was married?"

Bruce laughed, remembering Paul's description of his

ex-wife's mother. There had definitely been no love lost between the two. "Probably because she wouldn't have been safe around someone like you."

Paul shot him a disparaging look. "I'm sure she feels safe around a choirboy like you."

She probably did at that, Bruce thought, though he had to admit that the comment left him far from flattered. Margo gave every indication of being at ease with him, far more than he was with her. And yet she seemed intent on pushing the envelope right to the edge of the table and beyond. He wasn't really sure just what that was about, only that his reaction to her was in no way as minor as he would have anticipated. Or liked.

Something egged Bruce on to retort, "Don't count on it."

Paul looked at him hopefully. He was always in the market to meet beautiful women and this one had taken his breath away. "Any chance of an introduction?"

The request rankled him. It shouldn't have. He had no designs on the woman, though he did feel protective of her inasmuch as she was Melanie's mother.

"Not on your life. It'd be like putting veal chops in front of a wolf." Bruce thought that over. "Although, in this case, I think the veal could pretty much hold its own." As a matter of fact, he was sure of it. Margo probably would have laughed at his Sir Galahad reaction.

Paul's eyes had lit up. "A feisty woman. Even better. I like feisty women."

"You like breathing women," Bruce corrected.

Paul grinned. "Makes it more interesting. But, hey, look at you." He gave Bruce's shoulder a friendly punch. "You've been holding out on me." Grabbing a chair, he pulled it around until it was at Bruce's elbow, then straddled it. "So? Tell me everything. Have you two—"

There was no way Bruce was about to serve Margo up for dissection. He changed the topic abruptly. "Just how soon do I need to get started with those lessons, or don't you know?''

Paul feigned umbrage at the lack of faith. "Of course I know. My educated guess is yesterday. Weston wants someone with the right image to represent our interests overseas." He shrugged, though it was evident that it did perturb him a little. "I couldn't make him change his mind, so I guess you're elected."

"Italy." Bruce rolled the word around on his tongue. It didn't make it any more palatable. He really didn't feel like uprooting himself right now. Ten years ago he would have thought the assignment a godsend. Now, it was an intrusion. He had renewed his relationship with his son, he had a brand-new daughter-in-law, and there were other reasons forming that made him want to remain exactly where he was. He didn't like the idea of leaving it all behind.

"That's the country," Paul agreed glibly.

Bruce knew he could always say no, but it did mean a step up in his career. "When would I have to go?"

Paul told him the rest of what he knew. It would all be made officially public within the next two days.

"That's still up in the air right now, but the Italian rep is coming here in four weeks. If everything checks out to everyone's satisfaction, my guess is that you'll be Florence-bound in about five weeks." Rising, Paul pushed the chair back where he got it. "Unless, of course, you turn him down, and then Weston'll have to pick second best."

They'd been hired within three weeks of each other. The only reason Bruce was ahead at all was because he'd buried himself in this job while Paul had continued to live a normal, active life outside the office. Still, he never pretended to pull rank. Except when he was getting back at Paul for getting on his case. "You'll get your shot when he's down to twenty-ninth best."

Paul pressed two hands across his chest, wounded. "Ow, cruel, Bruce, very cruel. And here I thought you were so mild-mannered.'' He raised and lowered his brows like a latter-day Groucho Marx. ''Must be more going on with you and Mama-in-law than you're willing to admit.''

Bruce raised his hands in surrender, though he had no intention of giving Paul any more information, no matter what he said, threatened or pleaded.

''I'm sorry I said anything. Now go, I've still got work to do on this project.'' A thought had occurred to him as he'd been verbally sparring with Paul. He pulled the report from the out-box and opened to the next-to-last page.

Paul began to reach for Bruce's pocket where the photo lay only to have his hand batted away. ''Think she's ready to go out with a real man yet?''

Bruce never even bothered to look up. ''She already is. Don't let the door hit you on the way out, Paul,'' he murmured, writing in the margin.

He heard Paul laugh as he left the office.

''Margo would be perfect for it,'' Lance affirmed as soon as Bruce told him about needing lessons that evening.

''Margo would be perfect for what?'' Margo called out from the kitchen where she was making root beer floats.

They'd all spent the better part of the last four hours dismantling the furnishings she'd borrowed from the studio and returning them to the proper warehouses. It'd taken two trips to get everything back.

''Mama has ears like a bat when her name's mentioned,'' Melanie confided.

''What a lovely image.'' Margo shuddered as she walked into the room, carrying four tall, frosty glasses on a tray. Bruce rose to his feet and took it from her, placing it on the coffee table. She smiled her thanks before looking at Lance. ''So, what is it that I'd be perfect for?''

Bruce could think of a number of things, none of which he could share in present company. He had a vague feeling, though, that Paul would have been proud of him. Not that that was a sterling endorsement.

Instead, he turned toward her and said, "I need to learn Italian, fast. Do you—"

"Like a native," she assured him. She picked up one of the glasses and made herself comfortable on the love seat. "How soon do you need to get started?"

Bruce picked up a glass. "As soon as possible."

She took a long sip, letting the thick liquid cool her throat before saying, "Well, you're in luck. I'm available. The employment agency I've been working with hasn't called about any positions yet, so I'm all yours." She raised her eyes to his, her mouth curved in a smile that could be interpreted in as many ways as her words.

Suddenly feeling parched, Bruce tried to take a long sip and found his progress impeded by ice cream lodged in his straw.

"I'd pay you, of course."

The offer surprised her. "I couldn't take your money, Bruce. We're family, remember?" It seemed strange, having spent so much time strengthening her independence, that family could mean so very much to her, but it did. Had to be where she came from. You could take the girl out of the small town, she thought, but you couldn't take the small town out of the girl.

"It wouldn't be my money," he told her quickly, "it'd be the company's." He didn't want her putting herself out for no compensation. "They want me to learn Italian, and they're willing to foot the bill." He'd had his meeting with Weston by the end of the day and had been told pretty much everything that Paul had already alerted him to.

"Why are they so eager for you to learn Italian?" Melanie wanted to know.

He hadn't gotten to that part in his narrative. Bruce watched Lance's expression when he answered, "They want to send me to the office they're setting up in Florence.''

"Permanently?" Lance asked. They had so many years to make up for.

Bruce tried to read his expression and failed. "It's all up in the air right now. But the airplanes fly both ways, and even if it's a long stint, I can come home for visits.''

"Well, if your company's paying, that's different. I'll give you my corporate rate." She quoted a sum and saw the surprise that registered on his face. It made her grin. "I don't come cheap.''

He found himself smiling at the affirmation. "Now why doesn't that surprise me?''

Margo knew there had been companies that had refused to meet her price. Those were the companies she hadn't worked for. But she wasn't thinking of her reputation right now, she was thinking of a very compelling man who needed her services. The fact that it was only temporary made it that much better. No time for problems to arise and ruin things. "If they say no—''

"Yes?" Bruce fully expected Margo to tell him that she could probably recommend someone else to him whose rates were less expensive.

Margo took another long, languid sip before continuing. She'd never outgrown her love of the basics in life, and ice cream came under that heading. "We'll discuss a private arrangement." The idea of their working together intimately pleased her. "One way or the other, we can start when you take me back to the apartment.''

If he didn't know better, he would have said that she was straining at the bit to begin. "We came in separate cars,'' he reminded her.

The correction left her unfazed. "Then you can follow me." Margo looked around the room and sighed as she finished her drink.

Melanie studied her mother now. Margo looked almost

wistful. Was it because Bruce was going to Italy? Or was there something else at play here? Something more personal? "Anything wrong, Mama?"

Margo placed her empty glass on the tray. "No, I was just thinking how bare the room looks without the swords and the shields."

Though she loved memorabilia, and had loved indulging in impromptu fantasies this last week, of late Melanie had felt a desire to leave her own stamp on things. Hers and Lance's. "Oh, I don't know. I kind of like seeing the walls."

She glanced at the sofa they had put back just an hour ago. "The throne was nice."

"But there was only one," Lance pointed out. He and Melanie exchanged looks. They'd made love on it that first night, not even making it to the bedroom.

"Maybe I could—"

Lance held up a hand before she was off and running. In that respect, she was a lot like Melanie. He felt a little outnumbered. "No, that's okay. The sofa's fine. And it has all those fringe benefits, too." The throne had been nice, but there was a lot more room for creativity on the sofa.

Margo didn't have to ask what those fringe benefits were. She could guess just by looking into their eyes.

Bruce lost sight of her car. The low-lying fog had settled in like a thick boa along the city's streets, blocking his view of everything but the closest of objects. The low beams he thought belonged to Margo's car turned out to be the taillights of a BMW that had cut in between them.

Muttering a few choice words under his breath, Bruce passed the BMW and inched his way along until he finally arrived in front of Dreams of Yesterday. Thank God there was a streetlight in front of the shop, illuminating his way, Bruce thought.

She'd made it to the building ahead of him. It hardly

surprised Bruce. There were lights coming from the second floor, slicing through the fog like a razor-sharp light saber.

As he pulled his car up along the curb, the light shining from the window reminded him of a beacon guiding lonely ships in from the sea.

Was that what he was, Bruce thought, a lonely ship adrift, lost in the fog? He'd been out to sea for so long, he'd forgotten his way back. Or what it felt like to finally dock in a port.

He shook his head. Now Paul had him doing it, coming up with strange similes.

Getting out, Bruce shook off the encroaching mood. He couldn't let Paul's little routine get to him like this. He was fine, just the way he'd always been.

Or was he?

Was he really fine? Or was he, as Bess had once told him, just marking time?

A life was a horrible thing to waste, he thought, walking up to the side door. Maybe he should stop wasting it.

He felt his gut tighten ever so slightly as he raised his hand to knock.

It was a moment before the door finally opened in response to his knock. Combing back her hair with her fingers, Margo stood aside to let him in. As she did, the pad of paper she had tucked under her arm dropped to the floor.

Bruce stooped quickly to pick it up. He came face to knee with her bare legs and had the strongest desire to slide his hand along her skin.

Suppressing the urge, he forced himself to look down at the pad instead. She'd made an extensive list of different places. "What's this?"

She took the pad back from him. "'That' is our itinerary."

Had he missed something? What did going to the museum and renting videotapes have to do with learning Italian? "What itinerary?"

The smile she gave him was positively beatific. "The one we're going to adhere to while I'm teaching you. These aren't going to be stationary lessons, Bruce, where we gather around a book on a desk and absorb a bunch of words on a page. Language is a living, breathing thing. When I teach, it's a hands-on experience."

Which was, he thought to himself, exactly what he was afraid of. A hands-on experience. With his hands on her.

It was the first time, to his knowledge, that he had ever coveted a teacher.

"Come on." She linked her hand with his. "Let's get started."

He had a hunch they already were.

Chapter Seven

Bruce sighed. Feeling frustrated and somewhat foolish, he rose from the sofa. He was going to tell Weston no on Monday.

When he'd come over to Margo's after dinner, he'd expected her to just hand him a few books on Italian to let him get acquainted with the look of the language. Perhaps try out a few words in the privacy of his own home where, if he sounded like an idiot stumbling over letters that didn't look to him as if they belonged together, there'd be no witnesses.

Instead, Margo had insisted that they actually get started tonight. She called it getting his feet wet. He could think of another body part being involved in it.

Margo watched him as he crossed to the window. His shoulders looked rigid enough to land a single-engine Cessna on them. He was being hard on himself, she thought.

When it came to the lyrical quality of the Italian language, she had to admit that Bruce's accent was as flat as Eliza Doolittle's when she first walked in through the professor's door. But the professor's experiment had ended in success. As far as Margo was concerned, there was no reason in the world to believe that this would end any other way. He just had to have a little faith and a little patience.

By the expression on his face, she had a feeling that at the moment his quantity of both was far below the standard issue.

"They're just going to have to send someone else," he announced with feeling. Weston could send Paul in his place. "I'm not any good at this."

Margo got up and crossed to him. Standing behind Bruce, she reached up and placed her hands on his shoulders. Very slowly, she began to knead. It wasn't easy at this angle. It didn't help that he was as solid as a rock.

"Of course you are," she said soothingly. Bruce wasn't her first discouraged student. He wouldn't be her last. "Every baby is born with the ability to speak any language it hears. Are you going to tell me that a baby has a better ear for sound than you do?"

He turned around, taking her hands in his. "I've spent forty-seven years wrapping my tongue around English. It won't lend itself to another language now." Suddenly conscious that he was still holding her hands, Bruce released them.

Margo surprised him by taking one of his hands in hers. She drew him back to the sofa and sat down. But he felt too restless to join her.

"You must have studied some foreign language in high school."

A single shoulder rose, then fell, dismissing the detail before he'd even confirmed it. There was a framed panoramic scene of the chariot race from *Ben Hur* directly behind her. He stared at it. "Yes, Spanish." He didn't want to think about how that had gone.

Margo was pleased. The two languages were exceedingly

similar in sound and a great many of the words were close.
"Well?"

Hands shoved in his pockets, he turned to look at her.
"Badly. I studied badly. No, that wasn't strictly true. I studied a lot, I spoke it badly." He figured that part was self-
evident by his failure to mimic the phrases she'd tried to
teach him tonight. "I got through it by the skin of my teeth,
and I completely mutilated the language whenever Mr.
Feldman called on me for an answer."

A bad teacher could leave a devastating mark, Margo
knew. She had a feeling that was why he stumbled so badly
over the words tonight. "Obviously Mr. Feldman didn't go
about it the right way."

At the time, he'd hated sitting in Feldman's class, knowing he'd be ridiculed every time he opened his mouth. But
that didn't change the facts. "No, I just have a tin ear."

When she said nothing to argue the point, Bruce figured
that was the end of it.

He should have known better.

Margo got up from the sofa and walked into the next
room. Returning a couple of minutes later, she placed a
small tape recorder and several cassettes on the coffee table.
Still not saying anything, she raised her eyes toward him.

"What's that?" he asked suspiciously.

She gave him the answer in Italian, then smiled up at his
mystified face. "I figured you already knew what the answer to your rhetorical question was in English. Tapes and
a tape recorder." She spread out the tapes on the table.
There were five of them, all neatly labeled in her precise
handwriting. "These are simple conversational tapes. Long
playing." Picking up the recorder in one hand, Margo held
up the first of the tapes in the other. She extended both to
him as if she were entrusting him with the care of two
entities about to be involved in a sacred mating ritual. "I
want you to put these by your bed at night and play them.
One a night. The recorder is bidirectional, so it'll play the

tape over and over again until you shut it off—in the morning,'' she emphasized.

"I'll be learning in my sleep?" For a second he thought she was pulling his leg.

But Margo was very serious. "Sometimes that's the best way. Your resistance is considerably lower while you're sleeping."

He raised a brow. "You think I'm resisting?"

She swept the tapes into a small bag she'd brought out, then closed it.

"Well, you don't exactly strike me as being eager about this." But she had a hunch that was just his fear of sounding foolish. It would pass soon enough once he mastered a few basic phrases. From there his confidence should grow. "You have no idea what's awaiting you. Italy's a beautiful country."

He hadn't thought to ask her before. "You've been there?"

She recalled the experience fondly. "I spent five months in Rome. Walker Engineering sent me to teach its key personnel the fundamentals of the language. As a matter of fact—'' she smiled as the particulars came back to her "—to one of the senior engineers, Dale I think his name was, yes, Dale Hanna, swore he would never get the hang of it. He had this thick Texas twang that just poured over every word he uttered."

"And you got him to speak Italian," Bruce said dubiously.

It was one of her more satisfying accomplishments. "Fluently. I even got him to lose some of his twang, although it seemed to charm the Italians a great deal."

Margo smiled to herself as she thought of the country. There had been one fabulous, starlit night in Palermo she especially cherished. A fabulous, starlit night with a passionate man who had fine-boned, delicate hands like a gifted pianist. Carlo. She wondered whatever happened to him and if he was happy. She hoped so.

Her mind was elsewhere, Bruce thought, looking into her eyes. He felt oddly excluded and he found himself wanting to draw her back to this room, to him. He indicated the tapes. "And you used those?"

She blinked, coming around. "I used those," she echoed. "They came in very handy for my tougher students. I guarantee you'll be speaking like a native in four weeks. Or at least well enough for a native to understand you," she amended with a smile when he gave her a very skeptical look.

"Only if it's a very patient, understanding native, and I use a lot of sign language," he added. When she laughed, he felt some of his unwieldy embarrassment fade. And something else stirred in its place. It was time he left.

Bruce took the bag of tapes she handed him, as well as the tape recorder. "I guess I'd better be going. This looks like a lot to absorb."

"Like I said, one tape a night." She walked him to the door. "What about tomorrow?"

His hand on the doorknob, he turned, almost bumping into her. She stepped back, but there was still too little room between them. "Tomorrow?" he repeated. What was she asking? "Tomorrow's Saturday."

She laughed again. He made her think of a befuddled puppy. A large, lumbering puppy who was trying to co-ordinate all four feet at the same time. "Yes, I know. I have a calendar. I promised Melanie I'd work at the store until one, but I'm free after that."

Oh. She was asking to get together. Why was it that she always wound up taking the lead? And why was he so mentally clumsy every time he was around her? "Where would you like to go?" he asked belatedly.

She had an idea, but she didn't want to spring it on him

until she made a call tomorrow morning. "Somewhere where we can practice your Italian."

"I don't know any Italian." And he doubted, despite her stubborn insistence, that he ever would.

Undaunted, Margo tapped the bag of tapes with one pink-tipped forefinger.

"But you will. Don't forget, turn the recorder on before you go to bed." Unable to resist, she smoothed down one edge of his collar that threatened to curl up. "It'll be painless, I promise."

Something warm was unfolding within him, something he was having trouble ignoring. He continued trying.

He shifted the tapes. Margo seemed pretty certain that she could teach him, but he was far from convinced. He wasn't being modest when he'd told her about his Spanish class. How much more difficult would language lessons be for him now, when he really had no desire to learn?

He shrugged, his arm accidentally brushing along her breast. Heat charged up his body like Teddy Roosevelt taking San Juan Hill.

"That remains to be seen," he forced out.

"You can do it. I have faith in you." Then, surprising him, she brushed her lips against his cheek. The charge was completed. Roosevelt had taken the hill.

Bruce looked at her for a long moment, the velvet touch of her lips warm on his skin. "You would get me while my hands are full," he murmured.

Very deliberately, her eyes on his, Margo took the bag of tapes and the recorder from him. She placed them on the floor beside his feet.

"They're not anymore," she said quietly.

"So they're not." His heart began to pound as he took her into his arms. "You do have a way of plowing through obstacles."

She turned her face up to his. "Only when they shouldn't be obstacles in the first place."

Bruce brought his mouth down to hers, feeling more alive than he had all day. It was as if the entire day had been coming to this one instant in time, to this focal point.

He flattered himself that this time at least he was prepared for what was about to happen.

But even when you were prepared to be kicked by a mule, when the hoofs finally made contact, the jolt was still there. You still went flying.

And so it was with her kiss. She sent him flying. The only difference was, this time he knew the trip was coming. This time he was more willing to enjoy it. And maybe even eager to enjoy it.

His hands dove into her hair, cupping the back of her head as he deepened the kiss. And managed to give her just the tiniest bit of his soul in exchange for the gift she was giving him.

Rising on her toes, Margo leaned into him, letting herself get lost in the magic his mouth wove. She began her freefall in space, confidently anchored to only one thing. The word *temporary*.

This was just temporary.

He was leaving. She was leaving. This was to be savored and enjoyed for what it was. A moment in time. A moment where she was free to enjoy every nuance, every fragment of what was happening to her because there were no consequences waiting on the other side. No pain.

She moaned as she absorbed the pleasure, the excitement charging through her. Pleasure and excitement he created.

Her moan echoed in his brain, fanning the flames of his desire.

Bruce found himself in the grip of an emotion that was almost intimidating in its strength.

The kiss deepened, taking them both to the center of something larger than either one of them had ever encountered before. Something infinitely sweet yet passionate and overwhelming for all that.

When Bruce drew reluctantly away, he had the comfort of seeing that she appeared as shaken as he did.

At least he wasn't the only one who felt as if he'd just gone running barefoot through the hot springs. It took him a moment before he could talk. He found it was hard to form words when his heart was hammering loud enough to rival a pneumatic drill.

Margo drew a deep breath. That had been more exhilarating than a forty-story drop on a roller coaster. She made no attempt to hide the effect Bruce's kiss had on her. Instead, she exaggerated it by pretending to fan herself. "Well, you kiss well enough to pass for an Italian."

Just when Bruce thought he'd turned down another corner, she amused him again. It seemed that all the corners led back to her. "They have kissing standards?"

Margo nodded solemnly. "From novice all the way up to wow-better-carry-your-own-fire-extinguisher." Drawing another breath, she let it out more slowly this time. She found it just the tiniest bit disconcerting that her pulse was still doing some very erratic things. "I suggest you stand very close to a fire hydrant when you kiss a woman over there. And then get ready to run like hell if any of her family shows up. They take kissing very seriously in Italy." She winked.

"So do I." Bruce shook his head, his feelings still a shade jumbled as he tried to set them in order and pull them away from the direction they seemed to be going in. "I'll be too busy working to be doing any kissing once I get there."

He didn't mean that, she thought. Not with a mouth like that. The women would be all over him. "One should never waste a natural talent."

He cupped her cheek, fighting a silent, intense war with himself. Part of him, a very new, unfamiliar part, wanted to remain here. To explore the sensations that this woman seemed to generate within him, with her laughing eyes and her soft mouth.

But the practical side, the part of him that had been in charge of his survival for all these years, won the tug-of-war.

Dropping his hand to his side, Bruce bent down to pick up the tapes and recorder from the floor. "I'll stop by the shop at one."

"I'll be there," she promised.

Margo had to admit that she was surprised he was leaving. She tasted raw desire on his lips. And his body, hard and lean, had certainly given her every indication that he was willing to remain a while longer. Apparently, when it came to him, she was not as good at reading signs as she usually was. And as she closed the door behind Bruce, it bothered her a little that her knees felt curiously weak.

Stopping just long enough to deposit the tapes and recorder on his bed, Bruce stripped off his clothes and went into the shower stall. Turning up the cold water, he stood under its hard, needlelike spray until the throbbing yearning abated.

He stood there a long time.

Finally, knowing that if he remained any longer he would single-handedly start another water shortage, Bruce shut off the shower. He rubbed the towel hard against his skin, silently lecturing that he had no business letting himself feel this way.

But it wasn't a question of "letting" himself feel. He wasn't in charge here. There was no denying the fact that whether he liked it or not, Margo McCloud was encroaching on his territory, slipping in through cracks he hadn't, until she came into his life, been aware were there. Now she lingered on his mind like a fragment of a song that refused to fade away no matter how many thoughts he attempted to crowd in to oust it.

His torso wrapped in a towel precariously anchored at his hip, he padded into the kitchen and poured himself a glass of Chablis. The wine was meant to help him unwind, but it fell painfully short of the mark. It did nothing to mute the haunting refrain that was Margo.

If anything, it enhanced it.

Giving up, he decided to go to bed. It wouldn't hurt to get a good night's sleep for a change.

Dutifully, just before he climbed into the bed that always felt far too big to him, Bruce placed the recorder on the nightstand beside the telephone. He popped the cassette labeled Number One into the machine.

Bruce frowned. He had his doubts just how successful this method was going to be. There'd been nights when he fell asleep over his work with the television set on. Yet he'd never woken up with an overwhelming urge to crack wry political jokes like the late-night talk show host he'd been listening to when he fell asleep.

Still, Margo earned her living at this, so she had to know what she was talking about. He owed it to her to give this a chance before rejecting the exercise.

Getting into bed, he leaned over the recorder and pressed the Play button.

"Buon giorno. Good morning."

Bruce sat up, hitting the Stop button. He'd expected to hear the disembodied, artificially cheerful voice of some anonymous male or female going over the basics of the language. He had in no way been prepared to hear Margo's voice in his bedroom. From the very first syllable, Margo's whisky-dipped voice had filled the room, nestling in the corners and totally blanketing him with its throaty sensuality.

How the hell was he supposed to fall asleep listening to that?

It wasn't the kind of voice that lulled you to sleep. If

anything, it was the kind of voice that crept into your dreams and roused you awake.

Any good the shower had done was completely negated.

Bruce stared accusingly at the machine. If he didn't know any better, he would have said it was daring him to turn it on again.

He had to be losing his mind. A forty-seven-year-old man, and he was imagining a game of chicken pitted against a tape recorder.

The absurdity of that aside, what was he going to say to Margo tomorrow when she asked if he'd followed her instructions? That he'd balked at hearing her voice in his bedroom? This time, he knew he wouldn't appreciate hearing the sound of her laughter, because it would be at his expense.

He couldn't tell her that, and he refused to lie and say he'd played the tape, not when he didn't know what was on the rest of it. Bruce supposed he could get up tomorrow and just play it then, but that wasn't the point of it, was it? The point was to get the sound of the words into his subconscious.

Just as she had gotten into his subconscious. With little to no effort at all.

Steeling himself, he pressed the Play button again, then reached over to shut off the light.

As he lay back on his pillow, staring at the ceiling, he decided it wasn't humanly possible to steel himself as much as he'd need to.

Her voice came to him in the dark like a gentle lover, drifting over his body and seeping into his mind. Taking him prisoner.

Melanie stole a look in her mother's direction. Dreams of Yesterday was enjoying an unusual spate of business this morning. So much so that she hadn't found three minutes to string together to talk to her. It wasn't even the number of customers, it was just that they seemed to insist on coming into the store single file, one on the heels of the other. Without Joyce, who'd gone on vacation, to assist, one or both of them were required to remain on their toes and busy.

She'd never thought she'd live to see the day that business got in her way. But it did today. She had questions she wanted to ask, questions she couldn't ask with strangers hovering around.

Finally, just before one o'clock, the ongoing traffic within the shop experienced a lull.

Taking advantage of it, Melanie approached her mother. She attempted not to sound as if she was eager to hear a report.

But she was. "So, tell me. How did the language lesson go last night?"

Margo had just been thinking about that, wondering if Bruce was going to show up or find a handy, last-minute excuse to cancel. He'd looked so adorably uncomfortable, trying to mimic her accent as he repeated the words she told him.

He was a man who did "adorable" well.

"He doesn't think he has a knack for it. But I think he's too hard on himself." Out of habit, she glanced at her watch, though she'd just done that a couple of minutes ago. "He's coming by at one and we're going to get started for real this time. He doesn't know it yet, but we're going to take in a matinee of *Tosca.*" She'd just called the Performing Art Center and was told by a beleaguered clerk that the box office still had tickets available for the 3:00 performance.

"You're dragging him to the opera?" Melanie could just hear Lance's response to that if she asked him to go with her.

"I'm *taking* him to an Italian opera," Margo corrected. Bruce was far too powerful a man to drag anywhere. "I want him to know what it feels like having the words surround him.''

Her mother's reasoning mystified her. Even she didn't care that much for the opera, and she loved musicals. She was certain there was some unwritten law somewhere that said men and operas did not mix. Still, her mother seemed set on it.

"And this method works?"

Margo looked surprised that Melanie doubted her. "I've never had any complaints."

Melanie grinned. No one would ever complain to her mother about her ways. Everyone liked her too much. "You haven't told me what you think of him," Melanie prodded, glancing at the door. Afraid that someone would walk in, ending the conversation before it started getting interesting.

"Sure I did." Margo stopped to straighten a row of photographs that had shifted ever so slightly. Must have been a tiny tremor during the night, she mused. She'd almost forgotten that earthquakes, especially small ones, were a way of life here. "I told you he was gorgeous." She glanced at Melanie over her shoulder, an understanding smile on her lips. "Of course, that was on your wedding day, and you could be forgiven for having had other things on your mind."

Melanie moved so that she could face her mother while the other woman fussed over the frames. "I'm not talking about his looks, Mama. What do you think of him? Of Bruce, the man."

That was an apt way to describe him, Margo thought. Bruce, the man. He certainly was that, all man. Maybe even a tad more than she bargained for, although, in the long run, she could always hold her own, she assured herself.

"He's very nice. *Very* nice." She leveled a look at her daughter. "Just what is going on in that mind of yours?"

"Nothing," Melanie assured her. Even to her own ear,

that came out more quickly than she'd anticipated. "Mama, have you ever thought about settling down?"

This was new, Margo thought, surprised. Melanie had never once suggested that she change her way of life, not even when she was a lot younger. "You mean not traveling around from country to country?"

Melanie shrugged that part away. It wasn't the heart of the matter. "Yes, that, and settling down with someone."

Margo bit the inside of her cheek to keep her smile from surfacing. "You want me to move in with you and Lance? I don't think he'd like that."

Melanie pinned her with the same look that she'd used countless times before. "You know what I mean."

"Yes, I do, and no, I don't." She moved past her, looking for something else to keep her occupied before Bruce arrived or another customer materialized. She didn't kick back easily. "Think of settling down," she added. "Why should I?" Now that Melanie was grown and taken care of, she liked moving from place to place, never staying long. Never being hemmed in. "I get to travel, meet fascinating people, make friends all over the world and get paid for it." She turned around to look at Melanie. "I can't think of anything better than that."

All this time, Melanie had never thought of her mother as being unhappy, never thought of her mother as running from something. Now she wasn't that sure. "I can."

Margo knew exactly where she was coming from. Melanie was thinking of her own life, the new one she had. It was exactly what she'd wished for her daughter. It just didn't work for her. She gave Melanie a quick hug. "That's because you're a newlywed and because you're in love."

Melanie searched her mother's face, not quite sure what she was looking for. Only that she would know it if she saw it.

"I want that for you, Mama. I want you to have this wonderful feeling, too."

Melanie had a good heart, Margo thought. She fervently prayed it would never be hurt. Or broken the way hers had been. It had made her stronger, but at a price. "You can't just send out an order for love, the way you can for pizza." She shrugged, trying to sound blasé. She didn't want Melanie wasting her time worrying about her. Not now, after all these years. Her life's promise was just beginning to be fulfilled. "Some of us don't find lasting love."

Fueled by concern and the power that newfound love provided, Melanie wasn't prepared to give up the subject just yet. "You might if you open yourself up to the possibilities."

Possibilities, real possibilities, carried a downside to them. She'd been hurt by the first two men she'd ever placed her faith in. Her father and Melanie's father. She wasn't about to go down that route again. Her method was far better and far less hurtful.

"I'm happy just watching you be happy." The chimes at the front door sounded, announcing another customer. Relieved that the conversation was indefinitely tabled, Margo turned to greet whoever walked in.

And then she smiled. "Speak of the devil."

Chapter Eight

In Melanie's opinion, the "devil" looked very tired. She glanced at her mother, wondering if perhaps there was more going on here than her mother was willing to share for once. Had she and Bruce spent at least part of the night together? Both were very vital, dynamic people in their own way, and she'd already mentioned to Lance that she thought there was a certain chemistry between the two.

But if they had spent the night together, her mother would have looked at least a little tired, wouldn't she? Boundless energy notwithstanding, there was no reason for Bruce to look as if he'd been up half the night while her mother was the picture of freshness.

Melanie came around the counter to greet him. She brushed a kiss against his cheek, then stood back. "Are you all right, Dad?"

Bruce had no desire to explain to Melanie that the reason he looked like hell warmed over was because her mother's voice had haunted him all night. That didn't sound right, no matter how he said it.

Smiling genially, Bruce waved away Melanie's concern.

"I'm fine, just burned a little too much midnight oil last night, that's all."

Maybe they *had* spent the night together, Melanie thought. That might account for her mother's exuberance this morning, although with Margo, it was usually difficult to differentiate between her natural energy and if there was something special going on.

Was something special going on? She felt curious enough to burst, but there was no tactful way to ask when they were both here.

Anxious to be alone with her so he could question her, Bruce looked at Margo. "Ready to go?"

Purse in hand, she was already slipping her arm through his. "I've been counting the minutes."

The funny thing about it, though the remark was playful, Bruce half believed her. There was something in her eyes that made him feel she'd been waiting just for him. But that, he knew, was part of Margo's charm. To make everyone feel as if they were special.

Trouble was, a man could let himself get accustomed to that feeling. More than that, he could learn to like it. Bruce knew he was going to have to watch that.

"I'll see you on Monday, Melanie," Margo promised.

Sooner than that if she could help it, Melanie thought, as she watched them walk out of the shop.

"You do look a little tired," Margo agreed as Bruce opened the passenger door for her. She slid in, waiting for him to join her.

Rounding the hood, Bruce got in on his side and started the engine, but left it idling. He realized he had no destination as of yet, but there was something more pressing to clear up first. The reason behind his near insomnia.

"Why didn't you tell me that your voice was on the tapes?" He tried not to sound accusing, but wasn't easy.

"I'm sorry, I just assumed you knew. Just take Main heading north, I'll tell you where to turn," she said in an aside, since he made no attempt to leave. "My handwriting was on the labels," she pointed out.

He pulled away from the curb. There was little traffic. The U-turn within the center island was simple enough to execute. "I thought they were just copies of language tapes."

With a flourish befitting an actress from the silent era, Margo dramatically placed both hands over her heart as she widened her eyes.

"Are you accusing me of performing an illegal activity? The FBI takes a very dim view of that sort of thing, you know. It's right up there ahead of stealing a pen from the post office." Dropping her hands, she peered at his face. His jaw looked tense. She didn't understand why the fact that she made her own language tapes should bother him. "Why? Did you have a problem with the tapes?"

He thought of shrugging the conversation away, but he'd come this far, he might as well admit to the rest. "I didn't have a problem with the tapes, I had a problem with sleeping." He paused, wondering if he should be telling her this. "Yours isn't the kind of voice that lulls a man to sleep."

A smile played along her lips. A smile that had insisted on infiltrating all of her. Slowly.

"Is that your roundabout way of saying I'm not boring?" Margo knew she was fishing for a compliment, but just this once, she indulged herself.

"No." Bruce had no idea why he felt so angry about the whole incident, but he did. Containing the anger took an effort. "That's my roundabout way of saying you have the sexiest voice I've ever heard, and I was up half the night, listening to it."

He bit off the words, making it a backhanded compliment. Margo didn't stop to analyze why it gave her such a thrill, she just enjoyed the feeling.

"Next time, try a warm shower."

Wrong, he thought. Looking down, he realized his hands

were tightening on the wheel. With effort, he forced himself to relax. There was a tug-of-war going on inside him again, and he had no idea which side he was rooting for. Which side he *should* be rooting for.

"A warm shower," he grumbled, "was the last thing I needed."

She pressed her lips together. This wasn't the time to laugh. Struggling to keep a straight face, she asked, "Did anything on the tape manage to sink in?"

Bruce blew out a breath and thought before answering. "Around the third time, I began chanting the words like a mantra."

She nodded. That was all she wanted to know. Actually, it wasn't. She wanted to know where those sexy thoughts of his had taken him, but that would be asking for trouble and she had a lesson to teach. "Whatever works. Ready for a little culture?"

He spared her a quick look, raising one brow. "Italian?"

Her expression was pure innocence. "What else? Turn left at the next light." She pointed.

"That's Sunflower." His brow narrowed. "Are we going to the Performing Art Center?"

She nodded, hoping he didn't know what was playing. Or, if he did, that he wouldn't balk. "Best place to pick up some culture."

All around him, the audience sat in what seemed like mesmerized rapture as they listened to the swelling of loud music and louder voices coming from the stage.

Though the house lights were down and the stage bathed in a dimness that was to simulate night, Bruce felt a headache forming behind his eyes. Its formation had begun the moment he'd taken his seat. He'd entered reluctantly, in deference to Margo's wishes, but was convinced he was going to suffer for it. He'd never been to an opera before, but he figured the same principle applied to it as to attending a hanging. He didn't have to go to know he wouldn't like it.

During a merciful lull between the uproar of operatic exchanges, he leaned over and whispered into Margo's ear. "This isn't what I had in mind."

She tried not to react as his warm breath slid all along her skin, heating it. Heating her. Employing a tremendous amount of control, she turned to look at him. "What did you think I meant when I said culture?"

Bruce shrugged. To be truthful, he'd been too preoccupied with the effect her tape'd had on him to give the latter much thought when she first mentioned it. "I had a vague notion that maybe you were going to take me to an Italian restaurant."

Amused and feeling for him, Margo patted his hand. "That's cuisine, not culture. We'll get around to that," she promised. "I know this wonderful restaurant where the menu's in Italian."

"We're not going there soon, I hope." With his luck, he was bound to make a mistake. Bruce could just picture himself ordering the chef or something equally embarrassing.

Behind them a woman cleared her throat very distinctly. When they turned in unison to look at her, she glared at them, her message clear: cease talking or leave.

Bruce saw laughter in Margo's eyes as she struggled to keep it from her lips. The kaleidoscope of women he'd been witnessing amazed him. One moment she was a sophisticated woman, bent on exposing him to Italian opera, the next, she was a giggling schoolgirl, caught passing notes in class. And then the next, she was a passionate woman, all steamy sex and promise, wrapped in humor.

Which was the real Margo?

As he settled back to endure the remainder of the act, Bruce had a feeling that the answer was all three. It made a man feel overwhelmed.

By the time intermission arrived, he felt like a death row inmate who had just gotten a temporary reprieve from the governor. He all but led the outpouring patrons in the retreat to the refreshment counter. He ordered wine for both of them, wishing he could get his hands on something just slightly harder to help him through the remainder of the performance...and through sitting so close beside her in the dark.

Ever since he'd lain awake last night, listening to her say the most innocuous phrases and making them sound as if she were making love to him with just her voice, his thoughts had taken a definite detour away from learning the language. They were now veering into territory that was far rockier than learning how to pronounce strange-looking words.

"So, do you like it so far?" Margo asked as soon as he found her sitting at a little table in the second-floor lobby. She watched his eyes as she swallowed her first sip of wine, knowing that if he lied, she could probably detect it.

He wasn't sure if she wanted the truth or not. "Do I get points off if I say no?"

Margo laughed and took another sip. She'd no idea she was this thirsty. "I'm not grading you, Bruce. I'm just here to help you learn any way I can."

Old habits were hard to break. He'd always thought of teachers as "them" and education, until college, had always been a matter of "them" against "him." But in this case, they were a unit, not adversaries meeting over pronouns and adverbs.

And maybe their being a unit was what was bothering him, he thought.

"Then the answer is a qualified maybe. I liked it better than I thought I would, probably not as much as you think I should."

Was that what he thought? That because she was a female, she liked the opera? In that case, the joke was on him. "I don't think you should like opera. *I* don't like opera."

He scowled. She'd managed to lose him without taking a single step. "Then why did we go? Why are we still here?" He was ready to make a break for it if she was.

She drank a little more of the wine. "Because opera's part of Italian heritage, and I wanted you to get a feel for it." She set her empty glass down beside his on a side table. The line was far too long for another. More wine wouldn't help, anyway. It wouldn't blot out this edginess she was experiencing.

"I can teach you the basics of the language, but in order to really get the hang of it, you have to let it seep into your system, let it become part of you. When I'm finished with you, you'll even be able to think in Italian," she promised. "And thinking in a language is a true sign that you've learned it."

His eyes swept over her. She was wearing a simple black dress, nothing impressive on its own. Yet on her, it was a designer original. She brought style to everything she did, as well as grace and more than a passing dose of sex. It made for a hell of a mixture.

"I bet you don't know what I'm thinking now." He would have put money on it. A great deal of money.

"That you wish you'd never started this?" Margo guessed.

"That's part of it, yes." He'd given it some thought and while the honor of heading the Florence office was considerable, it made no real difference to him if he were sent to Italy or not. He no longer had anything to prove, nor any need to bury himself in his work. He'd finally come out to see the sun, and he liked the way it looked. He wanted to keep on looking at it.

Margo searched his face in the moderately lit lobby. She was oblivious to the throngs of people around them. To everything else but the conversation she was having with Bruce.

"And the rest?"

He slipped his arm around her waist, and was amazed at how easily that came to him. And how right it felt. "That you are one hell of an incredible woman, Margo."

She turned her face up to his. "I bet you say that to all the women who torture you." The buzzer began to sound. Margo sighed, wishing that she had a little more time to watch this unfold. "Looks like intermission is over." She nodded toward the door. "Time to go in."

He eyed the entrance dubiously as the crowd shifted from the refreshment counter to the door. "Do we have to?"

She laughed, hooking her arm through his, just in case he had any plans of escaping. "Yes, we have to."

He sighed, a man resigned to walking the last mile, since there was no other choice.

"I was afraid you'd say that." But he allowed a great many other couples to get in front of them before he finally made it back to his seat with Margo. He was in no hurry to sit and watch for another two hours, all the while feeling his posterior fall asleep.

Bruce looked up in distracted annoyance when the intercom on his desk buzzed. Didn't his secretary understand English? He'd left strict instructions.

Containing a temper that was all too willing to flare up these days, he pressed down the intercom button. "Agnes, I said no telephone calls."

Instead of an apology, he heard a gurgle of distress in response to his admonishment. That was followed by his secretary's voice addressing someone else. "But you can't go in there!"

The next moment his door opened and Margo came in. Swept in was more like it. The woman could make an entrance coming out of the bathroom.

What was she doing here?

"This isn't a telephone call, Bruce," Margo announced needlessly. She set down what looked to be a picnic basket on his desk. "It's dinner."

Dinner. He was vaguely aware that his stomach had been rumbling off and on for the past fifty minutes. Still, there was no connection between that and her sudden appearance.

"Margo, what are you doing here?"

His secretary, very obviously upset by her inability to keep Margo out, appeared behind her in the doorway. "Mr. Reed, I'm sorry, I couldn't stop her."

Hardly glancing in her direction, he waved away Agnes's apology. He was far too taken with what Margo had on to pay strict attention to the other woman. He would have guessed it was spandex, but it was far too formal looking to fall in that category.

But it certainly took every breath right along with her. He'd never found himself so taken with the give of a fabric before.

"Don't worry about it. I doubt any force of nature could stop her."

Margo paused in her unpacking and looked at him, pleasure in her eyes. "Why, Bruce, what a sweet thing to say."

Agnes remained rooted in the doorway. The look in her eyes told Bruce she regarded Margo as no better than a plundering interloper. "Shall I call Security, Mr. Reed?"

"I'll let you know if I need them," he told her mildly. "On second thought, it's late, why don't you go home?"

Agnes looked unconvinced and unwilling to leave him alone with this she-creature. "I still have letters to type."

"Last pickup was hours ago. They'll keep till morning." He gestured for the woman to leave. Given no choice, she reluctantly complied. Once the door was closed, he looked at Margo. She was busy taking things out of her basket and placing them on the tablecloth she'd spread out on the carpet.

Puzzled, he crossed to her. "So, what's all this about?"

She glanced at him over her shoulder, then took out a bottle of wine and two glasses. "Your lesson."

Just how many things were there in that basket of hers? It reminded him of one of those trick cars they had in the circus, where seventy-eight clowns marched out of a small car.

"I called and canceled my lesson, remember?" he reminded her.

But Margo didn't stand corrected. Margo, he was quickly beginning to learn, had her own way of interpreting things. "No, you called and canceled coming over to Elaine's for your lesson."

Thinking of himself as a reasonably intelligent man, it never ceased to mystify him how quickly she could lose him once he was in a conversation with her. "Isn't that the same thing?"

"Not exactly."

She leaned over to extract a container of potato salad. He watched in fascination as the miracle of Lycra stretched before him. It just molded itself to her body like a second skin.

Margo sat back on her heels to look at him as she made her point. "I didn't want to stop lessons now, not when you were progressing so well."

He had to admit that when it came to studying a foreign language, he'd learned more from her in the last week and a half than he had in three years of high school. She was also a great deal easier on the eye than old man Feldman had been, as well.

But he couldn't afford to let lessons, even lessons he was taking because of the company, get in the way of what was really important to him: the completion of the project he was overseeing.

Much as he liked having her here, fussing over dinner if not him, she had to leave.

"Margo, in case you haven't noticed," he gestured toward his desk and its overflowing files, "I'm very busy."

"I noticed," she assured him. She rose to her feet in a motion so fluidly graceful, water would have been envious. "Your secretary took great pains to point that out." She brushed off her hands before reaching into the basket for the main course. "But you have to eat."

He wasn't about to argue that. Not when his stomach chose that moment to rumble and underline her statement. "I was planning on sending out."

Taking his hand, she coaxed him down to the makeshift picnic she'd arranged. "Consider this a takeout delivery. And while you chew, you can review."

It was useless to protest. "Food and poetry, what a woman."

Taking out the breadsticks she'd forgotten she'd brought, Margo offered him one. "Flattery is not going to get you out of this."

He cocked his head, studying her. Damn, but she was a beautiful woman. "What will?"

"Satisfying me." When she raised her eyes to his like that, he knew he was in danger of chewing on his tongue instead of the breadstick. "And I'll let you know when I'm satisfied."

He had an urge, just for a moment, to explore that statement in an entirely different context. To see if he could bring her to an entirely different realm of satisfaction.

Her eyes wicked, as if she knew exactly what he was thinking, Margo pointed to the platter of cold fried chicken she'd prepared. "All right, now what's this?"

With a sigh, knowing there was no way out, Bruce said, "*Pollo.*"

Like someone playing charades, Margo touched her fingers together and then drew them slowly apart, as if she were attempting to make him stretch out what he was saying.

He raised one brow in amusement. "It's a chicken made out of taffy?"

"I was trying to get you to say fried chicken." Laughing, she hit him with her breadstick. It broke, a piece falling into his glass of wine. He took it out and bit off the soggy end experimentally. He let the flavor dissolve on his tongue. "I think you might have stumbled on a new taste sensation."

She lifted a shoulder in response, letting it drop again. She had a way of making everything look so regal, so cool at the same time, that it brought the temperature of his blood up another degree.

"Wine makes everything better, and you're just trying to distract me."

"Why not? Turnaround is fair play and you certainly distract me." His eyes on hers, he dipped the tip of his index finger into his glass, then set it down. "Lean forward."

She did as he requested, but asked, "Why?"

"I'm going to test out your theory." Ever so lightly, he traced the outline of her lips with his index finger and succeeded in getting them both excited. He'd forgotten what it felt like, to feel this way around a woman.

His pulse accelerating to double time, he touched his mouth to hers. All it took was a touch and he felt himself intoxicated. There was no doubt about it, she made his head spin. Not a good way to go if he had work to do.

"You're right." He drew his head back, fighting off the temptation to kiss her again. "Wine does make everything taste better."

For just the tiniest moment, Margo had thought they were experiencing a blackout. And then she realized that it was only him. And her. When he kissed her, no, even before then, as he'd drawn closer with the promise of a kiss between them, he'd made the room fade away. Margo couldn't remember that ever happening to her before.

She wet her bottom lip with the tip of her tongue, tasting the wine. Tasting him. "You're sure about that?" she breathed.

"Maybe we need to perform a second test." He drew her onto his lap. "As a control."

She settled in, being just the slightest bit unsettled at the same time. Determined to ignore it, Margo turned a deaf ear to the disquietude echoing through her as she laced her arms around his neck. "As long as it's in the name of science, how can I refuse?"

He grinned. He liked holding her like this, liked feeling the weight of her body against his. "That's very noble of you."

"I try," she murmured as his lips touched hers again. The smile on both their lips melted into the kiss. And into something more.

And then the pinwheels started. The pinwheels that whirled and turned within her brain each time Bruce kissed her.

Except that they weren't pinwheels any longer. They were now the size of windmills. Windmills with long, powerful arms that stirred the forces of nature even as they were being stirred.

That worried her a little, that they were windmills now. Windmills were harder to control, not at all like pinwheels.

But this was only temporary, she reminded herself with fierce urgency. It was all right to enjoy this, to allow herself to sink in a little more deeply than she normally did, to allow herself to enjoy this man a little more than was her habit. There was no danger here. In less than a month they would be in two different countries.

There was no harm in kissing him, in letting her head swirl and her blood warm. No harm at all. It wasn't as if she would let herself get hooked. She wasn't the same naive, idealistic young girl she'd once been. She'd learned her lesson well.

And this was just recess.

Still, the strength of her reaction did threaten to pull her under. She splayed her hands against his chest, creating a wedge between them.

"All right," she said, trying very hard to catch her breath. "Enough procrastination. Tell me what we just did."

It took a moment for the roaring in his ears to subside. "Came very close to setting the rug on fire?"

Yes, there certainly was that, but it wasn't what she was going for. "In Italian."

His arms still tucked comfortably around her, Bruce shrugged. "I don't know how to say that in Italian."

Margo knew she should move back, create a little space between them, but she couldn't seem to make herself act on that thought. It felt too good being like this.

"How about kiss? Can you at least say that in Italian?" She'd given him a list to study earlier in the week and that had been one of the words on it. Surely he recalled such a simple word.

"*Baciare,* to kiss." He congratulated himself on remembering. Triumph faded as he looked at her. *"Danne un baccio, Margo."*

Nerves began to jump around within her like so many tiny tree frogs fleeing the security of their home as a fire threatened to engulf them. "Very good, but you have your tenses confused. What we did is now in the past. You're using the present tense for give me a kiss."

"I know," he said softly. Gently, he cupped her cheek. His eyes on hers, Bruce repeated the words. *"Danne un baccio, Margo."*

She could feel it beating. Her heart as it rose up and lodged itself dead center in her throat, she could feel it beating. Wetting her lips, she drew in her breath and laced

her arms around his neck again. "I believe positive rein-
forcement is in order."

"In Italian, Margo," he teased.

"In any language," she answered just before his mouth
took hers.

Chapter Nine

Bruce pushed back from the dining room table, afraid that if he didn't do it now, he wouldn't be able to get up later. He would have been hard-pressed to say who was the better cook, Melanie or her mother. More than likely, it was a draw. He was going to have to see about getting in some extra time at the gym to make up for the sinful way he'd indulged himself tonight.

Extra time. The thought almost made him laugh. It seemed like these days he didn't have any time, much less extra. What with the intense push at work to complete his project before deadline and the language lessons, he didn't have a spare moment to himself.

He had to admit that the language lessons weren't the hardship he'd envisioned. Smiling, he glanced at Margo sitting beside him. The lessons were turning out to be the highlight of his day. More accurately put, Margo was turning out to be the highlight of his day. She seemed to infuse everything she touched with sunshine and laughter. Especially him.

Up until a few weeks ago, he never would have guessed

that he could feel this way again. That he was even capable of feeling this way again. And yet, he was, he did, and it was all because of Margo.

He'd come a long way from the barren wasteland his life had seemed just a year ago. He had a family again, Bruce thought, looking at Lance. And he felt lighter, happier than he had in a very long time.

"Wonderful meal, Melanie," he told her. "Everything was excellent."

"It's not over yet." Melanie rose, picking up Bess's empty plate and placing it on top of her own. "There's still dessert."

Bruce would have groaned if it wouldn't have seemed rude. Right now, the thought of dessert wasn't as appealing as it should have been.

"Let me help you with those," Margo offered, reaching for Lance's plate.

But Lance was faster. "That's okay, Mom. I've got it." Picking up his plate, he piled his father's and Margo's on top of it. "Be back in a minute," he promised, hurrying after Melanie.

She was already depositing the dishes into the dishwasher. Taking Lance's pile from him, she lowered her voice. "Do you think anything's going on between them?" She indicated the other room with her eyes.

He'd been wondering that himself ever since his father and Margo had arrived with Bess. There seemed to be something, an intense electricity, buzzing between them.

"I don't know," Lance answered honestly. "Dad seems a lot happier, but don't forget, I don't have that much to compare it to. Still," Lance considered as Melanie put the finishing touches on the cake she had baked earlier, "there's this spring in his walk that only a woman can put there."

Dipping his finger into the bowl of whipped cream she was using as frosting, he popped it into his mouth. Melanie continued slathering the foamy confection along the sides of her cake with a spatula. Without missing a beat, she slapped his hand away when he went to take a second taste.

"Guess I'll have to satisfy my craving for sweets another way," he theorized, then stole a kiss from her.

Melanie merely shook her head as she spread a white glob across the top of the cake. "Is that the best you can do?"

Lance gave her a wickedly lecherous look. "Stick around after everyone's gone tonight, lady, and I'll show you the best I can do."

Bess cleared her throat loudly before entering the small kitchen. "I just came in to see if you two need any help with the dessert, since it seemed to be taking you so long." She eyed them. "But I guess I can see what the problem is now."

Lance laughed, giving his aunt a quick kiss on the cheek that succeeded in catching her completely by surprise. Though she'd been both mother and father to him for a number of years while he'd been growing up and she knew he loved her, Lance had never been outwardly affectionate.

What a difference a woman made in a man's life, Bess thought.

"All my problems should be like this," Lance told her as Melanie finished up the cake. He stole one last lick from the bowl as he placed it in the dishwasher.

Bess shook her head. "Between the way you two've been exchanging looks all evening, and the way they've been looking at each other," she nodded toward the living room where Lance had moved the dining table to accommodate everyone, "I'm beginning to feel like I should have brought someone with me just to have someone to talk to." The older woman narrowed her eyes as she pinned Lance with a look. He'd been acting like a cat that had just inherited an aviary all evening. "What's all the mystery about?"

"You feel it, too? About Dad and Mama?" Melanie prompted when Bess turned to look at her, puzzled.

Bess laughed shortly. "I'd have to be dead and buried not to. Those two are heading for something big."

Lance nearly dropped the plates he was taking out of the cupboard. "You mean you think they're going to get married?"

That was something he hadn't considered. His father marrying Margo. Would that make Margo his stepmother-mother-in-law? Was there a term for that sort of thing, other than complicated?

Bess had never known Bruce to move quickly. She shook her head. "I didn't say that, but there is a great deal of electricity bouncing back and forth out there. Sitting next to them, I'm surprised my hair isn't standing on end like Christopher Lloyd in the clock tower scene in *Back to the Future*." She winked at Melanie. She shared a passion for movies, both old and new, with her new niece.

"But your parents' behavior wasn't what I was referring to." Pausing, Bess looked from her nephew to Melanie. It was high time they came clean. "Now if you expect me to believe that this is just an impromptu dinner you decided to hold at the last minute, you're giving me far less credit than I deserve. I might be a lot older than you, but I am not senile." She could barely contain her glee. "Something's up, isn't it?"

"Maybe," Melanie allowed evasively, her eyes dancing. Because she was afraid she'd blurt the secret out before they reached the other room, she turned away. Picking up the cake, she started for the living room.

"Here, why don't you let me take that?" Before she could protest, Lance took the platter from her.

Bess smiled. That clinched it for her. "Don't worry, they don't break."

"They?" Confused, Lance looked down at the cake he was holding.

"Women in Melanie's condition," Bess explained patiently. "On the whole, you'll find that pregnant women are a great deal hardier than most men think they are."

Lance's mouth dropped open. "Pregnant? How did you—I mean—"

As if he thought he could keep this a secret from her. Bess laughed to herself. Everything about the way the two had been behaving tonight fairly screamed of it. Bess shooed him through the doorway. "Just get out there and tell them before I do it myself."

Melanie felt too good to be disappointed about missing a chance to spring her surprise. "You knew?"

Bess laughed, giving Melanie a warm hug. It was going to be wonderful, hearing the sounds of a child again. Widowed early, before she'd had any children of her own, this pregnancy of Melanie's was extra special to her. She could hardly wait.

"Not until just this minute, when you confirmed it. But let's just say I've had my suspicions all evening. Now move, boy." Bess all but pushed Lance out of the room. "I'm tired of standing here."

Lance noticed that his father and Margo were deep in conversation when they walked in. Their voices were low and intimate, with only soft murmurs drifting back to him. His aunt was right, there was something powerful going on. He was beginning to like the idea of having Margo as his stepmother. It was about time his father enjoyed the same sort of happiness he had.

Bruce straightened as the others walked in. "That looks delicious." Maybe he did have a little room left over, he thought.

Lance waited until everyone was back at their place. "Before we cut the cake, Melanie and I have something to tell you."

Margo couldn't hold back any longer. "You're pregnant." The words came rushing out of her mouth. Quickly she rose and came around the table to throw her arms around Melanie.

Her baby was having a baby. The lump that suddenly rose up in her throat threatened to choke her.

Lance's shoulders drooped a little as he looked from one face to another. "Isn't anyone going to let me say it first?"

He'd have thought that at least he would have caught his father by surprise, but Bruce looked as if he'd known all along.

"How did you know?" Lance asked, exasperated.

He knew for a fact that Melanie hadn't told anyone. They'd only just found out yesterday themselves and had spent the entire evening debating how to break the news to the three people who mattered most in their lives. Now, with mental telepathy obviously alive and well, it looked as if they could have been spared the trouble.

Bruce clapped his son on the back, trying vainly to hold back the torrent of emotion churning within him. Grown men didn't cry. "Hell, boy, you've been strutting around here all evening as if you're the first man who's ever successfully propagated his seed."

"Now there's a romantic and charming image," Margo commented wryly. She gave Melanie another quick, fierce hug before releasing her. "I ought to make you say that in Italian just to make you pay for it."

Looking very smug, Bruce proceeded to do just that. In perfect, unaccented Italian.

Looking by turns surprised and then extremely pleased, Margo applauded him. It looked as if her job was at an end. He'd learned even faster than she'd predicted. Once started, he'd become her star pupil.

In oh, so many ways, she mused.

It was almost all over, except for the shouting. Something within her felt a little sad, but she pushed it aside. Instead, she smiled at him. "I guess this means you're ready for Italy."

With each day that passed, he found himself resisting the idea of going more and more. "Ah, but is Italy ready for me?"

He'd loosened up a great deal from that handsome man who'd met her on the other side of the door at church over a month ago.

"They will be, once they lock up their daughters," Margo assured him. Her eyes shifted toward Lance. "Your dad's a very charming man when he gets going. Of course, he was a little reticent in the beginning." She leveled a telling look at her son-in-law. "I see where he gets it from." She put out her arms toward him expectantly. "Are you going to come here for a hug, or do I have to come all the way over there for it?"

With a laugh, Lance traded places with his wife and let himself be enfolded in Margo's embrace.

Rays of bittersweet sunshine shone all through her as she kissed his cheek. "You did good, Lance."

Mischief rose to Melanie's eyes. "Don't be that sure, Mama." Margo looked at her quizzically. "You realize what this means, don't you?" Melanie bit the tip of her tongue to keep the laughter back. "He just made you a grandmother."

Margo shivered. Having had no grandmother in her life, the term only had the most stereotypical connotations for her. "There's something very old about the sound of that." She looked at her daughter. "How many months do I have, to come up with a viable alternative to *'grandmother'*?"

Melanie nestled against Lance. "Eight."

That meant the baby had to have been conceived on their honeymoon. Margo suppressed a bawdy chuckle, but just barely. "Boy, you do work fast, don't you?"

His grandchild was going to have one hell of a grandmother, no matter what she finally settled on calling herself, Bruce thought.

"There must be some form of 'grandmother' in all those

languages you know that's acceptable to you," Bruce ventured.

Grandmother by any other name still meant grandmother, Margo thought. Which meant that she was getting older. It wasn't the process Margo minded so much, it was that she was growing old alone. There was never going to be anyone at her side, sharing life with her in every sense of the word, the way she'd once dreamed.

But that was all it had been, she reminded herself. Just a dream. Dreams very rarely became reality.

Or, if they did, she amended, looking at the way Lance had his arm draped lovingly over Melanie's shoulder, they weren't her reality.

"Yes," she said with a sigh, getting her mind back on Bruce's comment. "There must be. I just have to think about it."

She could feel her eyes misting as she looked at her daughter, at how happy Melanie was. Thank God she'd found someone like Lance.

Noticing the way her eyes were glistening, Bruce offered her his handkerchief.

But Margo waved it away, sniffing. "You know, the quality of air must have changed in Southern California since I was here last," she told the others as if she were making a scientific observation. "There's something in it that keeps making my eyes tear up."

Bruce slipped his arm around Margo's shoulders as he pocketed his handkerchief. "It's called happiness."

"It's called an allergy," she countered. Briskly, she moved away from him. "You sit," she instructed her daughter. "Let me cut this cake."

Melanie nodded sagely. "Good point, Mama. The knife must weigh all of three ounces."

Margo gave her a look. "I only hope your kid has the same smart mouth you do."

Melanie pretended to cower, covering her head with her

hands. "Oh, here it comes, the infamous 'Mother's Curse,' heaped on the heads of unsuspecting daughters from one generation to the next since time immemorial."

"See?" Margo looked at the others, vindicated. "What did I tell you? Smart mouth." Giving her the first slice, she kissed the top of Melanie's head. "Girl or boy, I hope the new little Reed is exactly like you," she told her with feeling. "Damn, there goes that allergy again." Margo blinked, sniffing.

Lance laughed, only to find himself looking down at a very blue pair of eyes.

"The primary rule, Lance," Margo informed him, "in Survival 101 is never laugh at a woman with a knife in her hand."

"Yes, ma'am," he said meekly.

"That's better." Margo nodded, slanting a look at her daughter. "He's trainable, I guess you can keep him."

The others, including Lance, laughed. As Bruce accepted his slice of cake, he decided that it was only his imagination that made him think Margo had become the slightest bit distant when he'd put his arm around her. She was certainly in form now.

Silence, something Bruce had become so accustomed to after Ellen died, now occupied the inside of his car like an uninvited stranger.

They'd dropped Bess off first at her new house, then had driven to Margo's apartment. It made him feel better to think of it as Margo's apartment rather than Elaine's, the way she referred to it. If it was Margo's, it meant that she had a permanent place she called home here. A place where he could find her if he wanted to. Calling it Elaine's always gave him the feeling that Margo was only visiting.

That any moment, she would take flight.

Never mind that it could and probably would still happen. He didn't want to think about it. He'd finally allowed himself to enjoy her company, really enjoy it. Bruce didn't want anything marring that feeling tonight.

But it was because he enjoyed her company, because he was getting to be so in tune with her that he realized that there was something slightly off tonight. Something was different. Interwoven in the fabric of her gregarious, outgoing personality was a thread that was a different hue, a different texture. It didn't belong, but it was there nonetheless.

Why?

He'd thought it was his imagination, like when the lights go off then on again so quickly that you begin to doubt your eyesight. Just long enough to make him wonder.

He needed to know.

Bruce pulled the car up to the curb beside the shop. Margo had been very quiet since they'd dropped Bess off. Granted it had only been a few minutes, but that alone caused him to be concerned.

He shifted in his seat to look at her. "Anything wrong, Margo?"

All evening she'd been experiencing this nervous flutter, as if things were slipping out of her hands, out of her control. Whenever she saw Bruce look at her, the response she felt tied her stomach up in knots.

Margo forced a smile to her lips. "What could possibly be wrong? My daughter and your son have just taken a step on the path to life's greatest miracle." Margo pushed the smile a little further, though she avoided his eyes. "And you're becoming fluent in Italian, something you would have sworn was a miracle just a little less than a month ago."

He reached for her. "No," he corrected, "the miracle here is you."

He wasn't imagining things. She had stiffened just then, like a laboratory mouse feeling an electric shock. The response did more than bother him. It hurt.

But he continued, pretending not to have noticed. "And you're wrong."

Trying desperately to ignore the jumbled feelings scrambling through her, she forced herself to remain outwardly calm as she looked at him.

"There's always a first time, I suppose." Her voice was appropriately breezy. Maybe she could have been an actress at that. "About what?"

He wanted her, he thought. Wanted her so badly he hardly recognized himself. He couldn't see, hear or smell anything but her. "About a baby being life's greatest miracle. It isn't."

"Oh?" The way he was looking at her made her melt. And freeze at the same time.

"Love is." Very slowly he ran his fingers along her cheek. So soft, so silky. "Finding love is. Margo, I—"

Alarms went off all through her as panic bit out large chunks of her soul. She didn't want to hear this. Margo jerked the handle down, opening her door.

She needed to get away before she couldn't.

"It's getting late, Bruce. I'm a little tired. Would you mind terribly if I just called it a night? You're doing so well, I don't think there's a reason for another lesson."

She was talking fast, like she was fleeing something. Someone. He caught her hand as she began to slide out. Margo was pale, and it wasn't just the moonlight. "Margo, what's wrong?"

She thought of pulling her hand away, of just running into the shop, but that was much too melodramatic. And cowardly. She refused to be a coward, and struggled to get hold of herself. Nothing was going to happen that she wouldn't allow.

That was just the problem.

"Nothing's wrong," she insisted. *Damn it, stop asking me questions, just let me leave.* "I just—"

With effort, he tried to read between the lines. It still

wasn't easy for him. "Is it about becoming a grand-mother?"

She began to deny it, then saw it as her way out. If she said yes, he'd be satisfied and stop probing.

"Maybe." She paused to examine her heart. Perhaps that had a little to do with her reaction, but not much. "I mean, I'm thrilled she's having a baby. Having Melanie was the most wonderful thing that ever happened to me." And she wanted that same experience for her daughter. "It's just that…" She blew out a breath. Life seemed too long to go by so fast. "I never thought I'd see myself at this point in my life."

He could understand that. Somehow the news had hit him in ways he hadn't anticipated, either. After years of feeling old before his time, he'd just begun to feel young again. Because of her.

"Nobody starts out saying 'I can't wait to be a grand-parent.' But it's a natural progression of life." He smiled into her eyes, her vivid, vivid eyes that all but enslaved him. "Of love."

She had it under control now, she told herself. Her feelings were all boxed and neatly wrapped up again. The momentary aberration was over, just a panic attack for no reason. There was no reason to feel as if she had to bail out now. Bruce would be leaving for Florence soon, and she had an interview set up with DataLinc about a position in Nice beginning next month.

Everything was fine.

Taking a deep breath, she smiled at him. "Of course it is. I guess I was just being silly and vain."

"Not vain," he told her. "No one runs to embrace old age."

What he said reminded her of Elaine. "My aunt never seemed to mind getting older. She said people forgave you things they held younger people accountable for."

He raised a brow, curious. "Such as?"

She grinned now, remembering. Elaine had been so vital, so alive. It was by following Elaine's example that she had learned how to live again. And enjoy the process.

"Flirting. Having affairs." She wondered if she was shocking him. He wouldn't have been, had he only known her aunt. Elaine would have liked him, she decided. Really liked him. "Aunt Elaine had an eye for men until the day she died. It's probably what kept her so young looking. Not a wrinkle on her. And she was in her seventies."

He couldn't help asking. Couldn't help, too, that slight shaft of jealousy that traveled through him. "Is that what's kept you so young looking?"

Margo looked into his eyes before answering. "It's in the genes," she said evasively. Then humor played along her mouth. "That, and I've updated my birth certificate a couple of times," she teased, wishing it were only that easy to erase time.

Bruce shook his head. "Age is just a number." It was more than just a saying on a greeting card meant to cheer someone up. He firmly believed it. It was how you felt that counted. And right now, he felt young enough to make some very foolish mistakes in hopes that things would eventually take care of themselves.

There was no denying, for Margo, that she liked the way he made her feel. Eternally young and sexy. "Well, in my case, it's never going to become a very big number. I just won't let it."

Bruce let his eyes travel over her. "From where I sit, you have nothing to worry about for a great many more years."

He was tempted to kiss her. Tempted to do far more than that. But he didn't want to risk seeing that look in her eyes again. Not tonight. He supposed that he was feeling just the slightest bit vulnerable himself. There were feelings within him he needed to sort out before he acted on them. Or let them act upon him.

He moved to turn the key in the ignition. "I'd better let you go."

No, she thought, she was going to go on her own, before she was "let" go. Before something happened to end what had been the most exhilarating few weeks in her life. With the most exhilarating man she'd ever met.

Being with Bruce had made her feel safe and desired all at the same time.

That was just the problem. Feeling. She'd learned a long time ago that feelings only tricked you. They painted illusions that weren't real. No man could really make her feel safe because no man was her protector. No man could be depended on to remain when needed.

She had to remember that. Hang on to it because the intensity of her feelings for Bruce frightened her. Somehow, when she wasn't looking, what began as a harmless flirtation had swelled, infused with affection, until it had turned into something that was very strong.

Something she was afraid she couldn't handle.

After next week she wouldn't have to worry about handling anything. Even if he wasn't bound for another country, she would be. She was certain of it. The references she had gathered from the other companies she'd worked for guaranteed her a position anywhere she wanted.

There was, she reminded herself again, absolutely nothing to worry about. And since there wasn't anything to worry about, she could afford to relax, to indulge herself just a little more.

As Bruce watched, Margo seemed to transform right before his eyes. So quickly that he became certain he *had* imagined the earlier episode. There was nothing really bothering her, he thought, nothing making her distant except perhaps the jarring reality that she was getting older. But in her case, older simply meant better.

"Maybe you should come up for that extra lesson." Her invitation lingered seductively in the air as she got out of the car. She leaned over, looking into the car. "After all, you don't want to take a chance on going blank at the party you're hosting."

"The company is hosting," he corrected, unable to tear his eyes away from her. Grown men didn't drool, he reminded himself. Unless it was completely unavoidable.

The Italian representative for their proposed foreign office was arriving tomorrow morning. Weston was giving a lavish party at the Ambassador Hotel in his honor. Never much for gatherings, Bruce wasn't looking forward to it. The only thing that was making it bearable for him was that Margo was going with him as his date.

Date. The word still amused him. Dating at his age.

"What's so funny?"

He got out of the car. "Nothing. Come on, let's go upstairs. My tenses are getting all tangled."

The look she gave him was sinfully wicked. "Is that what they're calling it these days?"

Taking her hand, his laugh echoed in the night air.

Chapter Ten

The doorbell rang as she was debating which pair of shoes to wear.

"It's open!" Margo called, slipping on the higher of the two sets of heels. They were the more comfortable pair, and she had a feeling that it was going to be a long evening. The front door opened and then closed again. "I'll be right out."

She was running behind schedule and that always irked her, but it couldn't be helped. The interview with DataLinc had run over, lasting far longer than even her most liberal estimate. The personnel director had been so taken with her qualifications, she had insisted on arranging an impromptu meeting with some of the people who would be involved with the Nice-based office over the coming year.

By the time she walked out of the building, the job was hers if she wanted it.

Margo hadn't made up her mind yet.

It wasn't as if there was anything keeping her here, she insisted. Melanie was well taken care of, and she could always fly home if there was any sort of a problem, or if

Melanie needed her. And she had always wanted to live in Nice.

And yet she hadn't said yes immediately. Hadn't wanted to say yes immediately.

The offer from DataLinc—the personnel director had insisted on putting it in writing—was in her purse on the bureau. A silent reminder that she had options again. A way out if she wanted it.

If.

Not if, she corrected herself, *when*. A way out when she wanted it. Why was that so hard for her to get straight?

Checking herself over in the mirror, Margo picked up the long, dangling pearl drops she'd given herself on her last birthday. A birthday she had spent alone, she remembered. By choice.

She was putting on the second earring as she walked out into the living room. Bruce was standing by her coffee table, frowning.

"Sorry," she murmured. There. Finished. "Didn't mean to be late."

She didn't look rushed, Bruce thought. What she did look like was every man's dream. She was wearing a pink-sequined dress that hugged her every curve as it caught the light, flashing it back at him. Damn near hypnotizing him, he thought.

"You're not late," he told her. "I'm early." That wasn't why he was frowning. It was her lax attitude that concerned him. "And don't you know better than to leave your front door unlocked?"

She found it rather touching that he worried about her. "I was expecting you, and I didn't want to rush to the door, half-dressed."

"I wouldn't have minded." He tried not to dwell on the image that popped into his mind. "It's a lot better than coming in to find you dead. I could have been a burglar."

"But you weren't, unless you're leading a secret life I

don't know about.'' She brushed a kiss against his lips. ''And besides, burglars don't ring doorbells.''

It was hard to stay annoyed with her when she made him lose his train of thought like that.

''Just keep your door locked from now on,'' he warned. ''This is Southern California, not some rural town in Utah where everyone knows everyone else.''

Her mouth curved in amusement. ''Obviously you've never watched too many movies, or seen *Peyton Place* for that matter,'' she said, referring to the classic melodrama about a small town with scandalous secrets.

''I never had much time to watch movies. Ones in English at any rate,'' he added. The other night they'd watched two Italian movies, one with subtitles, one without, when she thought he was ready to wing it. When he'd protested, Margo tactfully reminded him that the people he would be dealing with in Italy wouldn't come equipped with subtitles.

She merely shook her head. ''So much to teach, so little time.''

Margo reached for her wrap on the back of the sofa, but he had already grabbed it. As he circled behind her, he realized for the first time that the dress she was wearing was backless. He paused as he assured himself that his heart hadn't stopped beating. Satisfied, he carefully draped the wrap around her shoulders.

''There's not much to this dress, is there?''

She turned around slowly, smiling up into his face. ''Just enough to whet an appetite.''

Amen to that, he thought.

Tucking her small clutch purse under her arm, she took a closer look at Bruce. ''You look nervous.''

It was more like a case of being unsettled. She seemed to do that to him, no matter how ready he thought he was for her.

''That's only because you look so beautiful, I think

you've liquified my kneecaps.'' Opening the door, he waited for her to walk through first.

She could get used to this very quickly, she thought. That, too, was a danger.

"Well, not only have you learned Italian, Bruce, but you've also learned how to speak fluent 'charming.'''

Taking her arm, he walked her to his car parked at the curb. "I'm not being charming, I'm only telling you what I see."

Getting in, Margo was careful not to snag her dress on the seat belt as she buckled up. She turned to look at Bruce. He was wearing a different cologne tonight. Something male and arousing. She could feel all her pulse points coming alive. As if they hadn't responded to him already.

Dressed in a tuxedo, he looked particularly dynamic tonight. "And I see a man who could go very far if he wanted to."

"I'm already going far." He started the car, wishing they weren't bound for the hotel and the lavish party. He wanted her to himself tonight.

The feeling was becoming more and more familiar to him.

"They're sending me to Italy, remember?"

Margo settled back in her seat. "I meant in the company." He didn't strike her as a man who was content not advancing. Soft-spoken, gentle, he was still a man who knew what he wanted, a man with a presence about him. Men like that resided at the top.

He had no desire to get involved in the clawing and backbiting that was part and parcel of every push to get to the apex of the corporate ladder. The view from where he sat—Bruce glanced at Margo, at the way the bodice of her dress rose and fell with every breath she took—was just fine.

"I've already gone further there than I really wanted to." The traffic light up ahead was out. Cars in all directions were queuing up, turning the defunct light into a four-way-stop sign.

Margo didn't understand. He was one of the major CEOs at one of the top software design companies in the country. Considering the way the field was mushrooming, that was saying quite a lot. Didn't he want to be there?

"I thought this was what you were working toward, what you were aiming for."

"What I was aiming for was just to blot out all the pain going on inside of me. Spending eighteen hours a day at the job accomplished that to a degree. I guess advancement was just a by-product." It was his turn to go. "But the pain's gone now."

"Speaking of gone, shouldn't we be there by now?" The hotel wasn't that far away, even with the dormant traffic light. Bruce was driving inordinately slow. "You don't want to arrive late for this thing, do you?"

An enigmatic smile played on his lips as he slowed for a yellow light, stopping as it took its time turning red. "I don't want to arrive for this 'thing' at all."

He looked at her, his eyes touching her hair, her face, the tempting swell of her breasts. Would he really be missed if he didn't turn up tonight? There would be so many other people there.

But none of them would be heading the Florence office, he reminded himself. With resignation, he pressed down on the accelerator again.

"I would like to take you to some isolated little café that no one's ever heard of where they serve real coffee—not cappuccino, not latte, but just plain, black coffee—and have three musicians huddled in the corner, playing the blues all night."

"Three?" The smile on her lips rose to her eyes. "Not four, not two, but three?"

He nodded, turning at the next corner. "Three's a good number."

He was a very unusual man, she thought. Some might have even called him special.

"You're the expert on numbers," she conceded.

"Yes," he said quietly, slanting another look at her. "I am."

Bruce had never walked into a room before where the most stunning woman in the place was the one on his arm. He didn't have to look to know that every pair of eyes turned in their direction when Margo and he entered the ballroom.

When *Margo* entered the ballroom, he silently amended. He was just her escort.

He wanted to be more than that.

Funny how things changed. Most of his life he'd been a great advocate of status quo. But things, life, had insisted on changing. First for the worst and now, in these past few months, for the better. His son had reentered his life, then he'd gained a daughter-in-law, one who, even before the wedding, had become the daughter he'd never had.

And now, a woman had come into his life. A woman who made his blood heat and his imagination soar.

All these years he'd never thought that there'd ever be room in his heart for anyone else but Ellen. Now he knew that he'd been mistaken.

It was a hell of a discovery to make at his age.

So was finding out that he wasn't above being just the slightest bit vain. He liked the way men looked at Margo, with admiration and desire. Most of all, he liked the fact that she was with him.

When the other men looked at him, there was envy in their eyes. There was even a spark of interest in Weston's eyes, and the man had to be moving well into his seventies, if he wasn't there already.

Out of the corner of his eye, Bruce saw Paul standing over by the terrace. As usual, the man had brought an extremely attractive young woman with him. If he was running true to form, Paul was contemplating a little rendezvous for later in the evening, after the party.

But at the moment Paul's mouth appeared to have frozen in midword. He was staring in their direction. Bruce wasn't sure if he even saw him with Margo. Knowing Paul, all he saw was Margo.

The lights from the chandelier played seductively along her dress, all but caressing her body. Just the way he longed to do, Bruce thought.

"Doesn't take long for your magnetism to kick in, does it?" he whispered against her ear.

"It did with you," she countered playfully.

Bruce inclined his head, agreeing. "I'm a slow learner."

She laughed softly, her breath shimmying up to his cheek. "Not from where I'm standing."

Bill Wakefield, a senior design engineer was the first to descend on them, cutting off their access to the center of the ballroom and the guest of honor.

"Bruce, you've been holding out on us." Wakefield hardly spared Bruce a look as he all but devoured Margo with his eyes. "*Who* is this charming creature?"

He'd never cared for Wakefield. Now he knew why. "Bill Wakefield, may I introduce Margo McCloud. My tutor," he added.

"Ah!" Wakefield's eyes took another languid tour of her body. "You make me want to crack open a few books myself." His voice dropped suggestively. "Along with a bottle of vintage champagne."

She'd come across more than one Bill Wakefield in her time. He bore very strong similarities to Jack, right down to the way he flashed his smile, with an aim at dazzling her.

"Champagne clouds the mind when you're studying," she said, her tone mild, disinterested.

"Not mine," he assured her. "It sharpens everything about me."

There was no feeling in her smile. "How very nice for you."

It was Bruce's experience that Wakefield never knew when to back away. There were no surprises tonight. "I'm going to Rome this summer. Maybe I might need a few lessons myself. How would I go about arranging for those?" The look he gave her was both suggestive and pointed.

She slipped her arm through Bruce's, appearing to hang on him. Killing two birds with one stone. Instinct told her that annoyed Wakefield and pleased Bruce. "When you're ready for them, talk to Bruce. He'll know where to reach me."

Wakefield's lips twitched in a sly smile. "I'm surprised Bruce still remembers how to reach."

What a creep, she thought. If they weren't at a party, she would have told him so. But she didn't want to make a scene.

Margo felt Bruce stiffening. She didn't have to look at his expression to know that he was coming precariously close to defending what he deemed to be her honor. Beneath his gallant exterior was an equally gallant interior. She wanted to see neither get into an altercation on her account.

Tugging ever so slightly, she began to draw Bruce away before he carried out her fantasy and punched Wakefield out. "Bruce is a very surprising man. But I'm sure you already know that. And to satisfy your curiosity, Bruce remembers everything just fine." She deliberately purred the words. "You'll excuse us, but we have to go mingle. Don't we, Bruce?"

He merely grunted in response.

"Be nice," she chided, more amused now than insulted

or angry. There would always be Wakefields in the world. The trick was not to let them get to her.

"I was ready to flatten him," he told her.

"I know." She swallowed the playful laugh echoing in her throat.

Bruce looked at her, hearing what he just said for the first time. He'd reached six-four by the time he was fifteen. Because of his imposing size, he'd never found it necessary to become physical with anyone. But he'd wanted to this time. He wanted to know what it felt like to smash that perfect nose beneath his knuckles. "I never felt like that before."

She grinned. "I have to admit, there's something rather exciting, watching your nostrils flare."

His attention was all hers again. "They did not flare."

This time, she didn't bother holding back her laugh. "Yes, they did."

He loved that sound, he thought. Hearing it defused any rush of temper that threatened to overtake him. "They're my nostrils, I should know whether or not they flared."

"You didn't have my view," she teased.

"You know what Wakefield must think now," he pointed out. He didn't want people thinking things like that about her. Not when it wasn't true.

She nodded. "I know." That they were lovers. Bruce had held back, very obviously reining himself in even when, just as obviously, he'd wanted to let go. He'd done it, she knew, not just because of the memory of his late wife, but out of an old-fashioned sense of consideration for her.

His behavior only intensified the conflicting feelings battling within her. She'd always just wanted to enjoy herself and move on.

But it wasn't that simple. Not anymore.

For now she ignored it. Margo raised herself up on her toes and pressed a soft kiss to his cheek.

Bruce looked at her in surprise. It didn't seem to bother her, he noted, that there was a ballroom full of people around.

"My Sir Galahad."

"You were right," Paul declared, coming up behind them. His eyes were all but glued to Margo when they both turned around to look at him. "She is a real knockout."

Disregarding the fact that she was being referred to as if she were a trophy rather than a person, Margo looked at Bruce in surprise. "You called me a knockout?"

Though he'd thought it more than once, Bruce didn't remember actually using that term around Paul. "I—"

Paul jumped in verbally. And took the opportunity to place himself between them. "Maybe not in so many words, but that was what he meant. I've been his friend for a long time and I can read between the lines. He's ordinarily so quiet, I have to." He put out his hand to her. "Paul Giordano."

She recognized his name. "You're his best friend." She slipped her hand into his and made sure her handshake was firm, rather than the delicate one she knew he was expecting.

"And you're just the best," Paul pronounced with a sigh that was almost comical.

Bruce tapped him on the shoulder. When Paul roused himself enough to glance at him, Bruce said, "I believe your lady friend is waiting for you to come back."

"What lady friend?" Paul added. Bruce pointed to the woman who was looking in their direction. "Oh, yeah. Julie. Right." Chagrined, Paul laughed. "You'll excuse me, I have a little damage control to tend to." He looked at Margo hopefully before leaving. "But you'll save me a dance?"

"Sure she will. At the next function," Bruce called after him as Paul hurried back to Julie.

Margo made no attempt to conceal her amusement. "That wasn't very nice."

Bruce looked at her, feigning hurt at the criticism. "Just living up to my responsibility. Sir Galahad, remember? Paul's my best friend, but he's also a bit of a womanizer. I just saved you from having to endure dancing with a man who has more hands than an octopus."

"Very thoughtful of you." Was that a trace of jealousy she detected? "Does this mean that every dance with you will be chaste?"

"Only if you want it to be," he said quietly against her ear.

The shiver it sent up her spine was in inverse proportion to the volume of his voice.

"Reed, nice of you to show up." Weston clapped a hand on his shoulder, breaking the mood as he invaded their space. "And this is—"

"Ms. Margo McCloud."

The name was familiar to him. He'd been the one to okay hiring her. He would have asked for an interview had he known she looked like this.

"The tutor, yes." He took her hand between his own. "I hear from Reed that you do wonderful work."

So he'd been talking about her, had he? Pleasure slid through her like smoke curling from a chimney Christmas morning. "Teaching is very rewarding."

"To be sure," he agreed. Still holding her hand, he slipped it through the crook of his arm. "Once we have the office in Florence up and running, I'm going to need a full staff to man it. And I don't believe in going outside the company to fill positions if my own employees are up to the job. That means we'll be in the market for a teacher on location." Like a magpie examining a shining rock, he cocked his head and looked at her. "Interested?"

Ambivalent feelings fought for control of her, but Margo

kept the struggle from registering on her face. "Mr. Weston, I am always interested."

The dry laugh sounded very close to a crackle. "Something I never tire of hearing from a beautiful woman." Glancing around, he found who he was looking for. "Come with me, both of you. There's someone here I'd like you to meet."

Bruce knew who he was referring to. The guest of honor, Giovanni Marcello. They found the slender, dark-haired man in the center of the room, surrounded by several of the company's CEOs.

As they approached, the man's husky, deeply accented voice was the only one heard. Even stumbling over English, it sounded melodic. Bruce felt like a student about to take his final exam.

Weston waited for the man to pause. It wasn't long in coming. "Giovanni, I'd like to introduce Bruce Reed, who'll be heading our foreign office."

"Foreign to you, not to me," Giovanni said grandly with an indulgent smile.

Weston, mindful of the agreement yet to be cemented, was quick to agree. "Yes, of course."

"A pleasure to finally meet you." Bruce shook Giovanni's hand. He was spared one shrewd look before the man's dark eyes roamed to Margo, obviously very taken with what he saw. Introductions were in order. Bruce stepped aside to usher Margo forward. "And this is—"

"The most exquisite woman I have ever set my poor eyes on." The flattering words descended like flower petals floating on the spring breeze as Giovanni eased Bruce out of the way. He took Margo's hand and pressed his lips lightly to her knuckles. "Tell me, what is your name, lovely lady?"

Unimpressed, she gave her answer in Italian.

At the sound of his native tongue, Giovanni's eyes lit

up. "Ah, but you speak Italian?" His pleasure was unmistakable as he repeated the question again in Italian.

"A little."

Giovanni immediately launched into a profusion of words that swiftly left Bruce behind, like a man who had just missed boarding the train. Obviously he hadn't learned as much as he'd originally believed, Bruce thought grudgingly.

Margo, he observed, held her own during the conversation. There was no indication that she was the least bit confused as the words continued to flow swiftly in her direction. She answered Giovanni's initial questions, made appropriate comments on several things he said, and then, ever so politely, pointed out that with the exception of Bruce, the others didn't have a clue what they were talking about.

"Oh, but of course, you are right. Where are my manners?" he apologized, though it was to her rather than the others that he directed the apology. "It is just that it is not often I discover angels speaking my native tongue." Hope alighted within the almost black orbs. "You will be part of the office that we are discussing, yes?"

Pausing, Giovanni looked to Weston for confirmation.

"I offered her a position." And if this was what it took to cement negotiations between the two companies, Weston was willing to put pressure wherever it would do the most good.

Giovanni looked as if he believed it was a done deal. "And you will accept, yes?"

Margo had never liked being backed into a corner, even a lucrative one. She thought of the offer in her purse at home. Options.

"I will think about it," she agreed.

That didn't sound as if she was going to give him the answer he wanted. Giovanni, accustomed to getting his way both professionally and privately, moved a little closer.

"Is there anything I can do to perhaps persuade you? You have but to name it."

"Thank you." Her soft, sultry laughter drifted between them. "You are too kind."

"Eh, 'kind,' yes," he acknowledged. He beat his fisted hand once against his chest. "It is, as you Americans say, my middle name."

Behind them, the musicians began playing *Stardust*. She doubted either man standing beside her recognized it.

But Giovanni did recognize an opportunity when he saw one. He took her hand again. "You will do me the honor, yes?"

She found herself glancing toward Bruce, who reluctantly nodded, before she agreed. That had never happened before, she realized with an inward start. She'd never looked for approval before doing anything. She didn't *need* any man's stamp of approval before she acted.

Yet there was no denying that his feelings had become important to her. That made her uncomfortable.

Giovanni swept her into his arms. As if to deny what she was feeling, to deny an even stronger emotion that was trying to break free, Margo smiled up into his face. They let the music take them away.

"Great idea, bringing her along," Weston congratulated Bruce. "Did you see the way he looked at her?"

"Yes," Bruce said evenly. "I did." And he didn't like it.

Damn, what was happening to him? Jealousy wasn't in his nature. Neither was possessiveness. Yet he was feeling both.

He was going to have to get all that under control and fast before he completely scared her away. Margo wasn't the type to be charmed by either of those traits.

"This should cinch it for us," Weston was saying. "She seems to have really hooked him." He cackled, building on the comparison that had just occurred to him. "He looks like a fish that's positively eager to leap into her lap, even if it means dying.''

''I don't think it's dying that he has on his mind,'' Bruce muttered in reply.

Weston merely laughed, missing the fact that Bruce didn't join in.

Chapter Eleven

Bruce stood it for as long as he could, which was a lot longer than he thought he would. All the while, he counseled himself the way he would a friend. That what he was feeling was a childish emotion. That he and Margo and Giovanni were all mature adults and could act accordingly.

That was just the problem.

Right now, he wasn't feeling very mature. What he was feeling was adolescently possessive. He didn't want Margo in Giovanni's arms, either for dancing or for any other reason. Bruce wanted her in his arms. Exclusively.

And for that matter, he had no idea what acting according to their maturity might mean to Giovanni.

But he had a damn good hunch.

Giovanni Marcello was darkly handsome, suave and, from what Bruce had heard around the office and from Paul, the man was born to money. It made for one hell of a combination. A background like that lent itself to a certain laid-back, carefree enjoyment of the finer things in life.

Bruce was afraid that for Giovanni, Margo just might

come under that broad heading. And worse, she might even like coming under that heading.

He didn't want to chance that.

So as Weston stood by, watching him with more than a measure of incredulous disbelief, Bruce crossed the floor and cut in on Giovanni.

Reluctantly surrendering his oblivion to everything else around him, Giovanni looked over his shoulder at Bruce.

"Oh, but we have not finished our dance yet," he protested when Bruce moved to take his place with Margo. He gave no indication that he had any intention of releasing her from his arms, a place he obviously felt she fit in very nicely.

"That's the whole point of cutting in," Bruce informed him.

"There are rules for such things?" Still dancing, Giovanni looked to Margo for an explanation.

But it was Bruce who answered him. "There are no rules for cutting in, other than the couple has to be dancing. And that the person being cut in on gives way to the person doing the cutting." He looked at Giovanni expectantly.

Appearing to roll this information over in his head, the younger man finally gave in. "This language of yours, I must say it is confusing." Giovanni smiled as he looked up at Bruce. The smile the latter wore was strictly perfunctory. Giovanni saw what he needed to see. "But the feelings, they are not. I bow to your claim, Mr. Reed." Inclining his head, he withdrew.

Margo slipped easily into Bruce's arms. With a contented sigh, she rested her head against his chest. Was it her imagination, or was his heart beating just a little harder? Because of her?

A small thrill shimmied along her skin.

"Well, that went well," she murmured.

Bruce folded his hand around hers. He could swear he

felt her smiling against his chest. At least one of them was amused.

It took him a moment to collect himself. "Frankly, I don't care if it did or not. He looked as if he was enjoying himself way too much."

Margo raised her head to look at him. And saw exactly what Giovanni had detected. Bruce was jealous. Really jealous. She couldn't help being flattered.

"Isn't that the whole point of this party?" she asked mildly. "To get him to relax, to enjoy himself and then sign on the dotted line?"

"Yeah, but—" Bruce stopped, some of his anger dissipating like taffy after it'd been chewed for a moment. He looked at the matter from her perspective. The grin that slowly spread along his lips was self-deprecating. "I am behaving like the rear end of a horse, aren't I?"

"Not a horse…" Her eyes shone with amusement and sympathy. He didn't like feeling this way, it confused him, she could tell. "A pony, maybe." And then she smiled up at him. "Actually, I find it very sweet."

"I find it annoying." He was keenly disappointed in himself. He didn't want to even think about what she probably thought of him. "I'm not like this, normally."

"I wouldn't know."

He looked into her eyes, searching for a sign, for something he could build on. "I'd like to show you."

Her response was guarded. "How?"

If he noticed the change in her voice, the infinitesimal change in her body as it stiffened ever so slightly against his, he pretended not to.

"Why don't you take Weston up on his offer?"

If they had more time together, if she got to know him, then perhaps she'd see that this was just an insane, temporary aberration for him. Until she had entered his life, he would have said that he hadn't a jealous bone in his body.

He couldn't make that claim any longer. But it was something that he intended to get under control.

"And which offer would that be?" Her face lit up with humor again, the guarded manner gone as if it had never existed. "His eyes were saying things I don't think the rest of him could make delivery on."

Bruce had no doubt that Weston was entertaining thoughts of his own about Margo. Probably half the men in the room were. That, too, was something he was going to have to get used to. He only hoped she'd give him the chance. "The offer to come to Florence, Margo. To work for the company."

Come to Florence with me, he added silently. He had an uneasy feeling that if he phrased it that way, she'd say no. The odd thing was, he wasn't certain if she would say no because she didn't want to, or because there was something else in the way. Something he couldn't quite put his finger on yet.

Margo knew she wasn't about to say yes, even though part of her was tempted. She couldn't say yes. It would ruin everything.

But for the moment she played devil's advocate. "That would put me in contact with Giovanni on a regular basis, wouldn't it?"

"And me," he emphasized significantly. Bruce held her hand tighter, curving his other hand around the one that rested against his chest. "And don't worry, I'll take care of Giovanni."

She tried not to laugh. He looked so endearingly serious. "Does that mean if he comes on to me, he'll find himself sleeping with the fishes?"

"Not sleeping," Bruce denied, "but he might be taking a long nap."

She could just see Bruce, bare-chested, fists poised to pummel the much slighter man into the ground. It was all so hopelessly Neanderthal and she had no idea why it gave her such a thrill.

But she couldn't help grinning at him. "I love it when you get physical."

It took all he could do not to caress her face, not to press a kiss to each lid and lose himself in the fragrance that lightly swirled around her. Was there a dab behind each ear and another along the column of her throat? Would he taste it if he kissed her there?

Damn, but he wanted to find out.

"This is a joke to you, isn't it?" he asked softly. Was that because she didn't feel the way he did?

Or because she did?

No, it wasn't, Margo thought. Nothing Bruce did struck her as a joke, just touchingly amusing. There was a difference.

"You don't have to beat up men if they come on to me, Bruce. I can handle myself. I've been doing it for a long time." Far longer than she liked to think about, but for so long that she was accustomed to doing it, and very set in her ways.

"I know." This time he did indulge himself. With the tips of his fingers, he swept a wayward curl away from her face. "Maybe it's time you let someone else do it for you."

Something came to rigid attention within her. She couldn't give up control, not over herself, not even a little bit. She'd been holding on for so long, letting go was not an option.

"I wouldn't know how." Looking around, she realized that no one else was dancing. This was getting to be a habit for them, dancing when there was no music. Margo drew away from him. "The music's stopped."

The only music he'd heard was the sound of her voice, low, sultry, as she spoke. He still heard it.

Unembarrassed, he merely nodded. "So it has."

Bruce was going to say something to her she didn't want

to hear. She could see it in his eyes. Margo didn't want the evening to end, but it would if he asked her to come with him to Italy. Not with the company, but with him. She couldn't do that, couldn't risk it.

Damn, why did he want to spoil things?

"Let's get something to eat, I'm starved," she announced abruptly.

Without waiting for him to reply, Margo turned on her heel and went to the buffet table.

Bruce watched her walk away, wondering just what he had said to make her mood change course so suddenly. She looked almost spooked.

It made no sense to him.

Initially, when he had tried to keep up a barrier between them, she had appeared to take it as a personal challenge. In very short order, she had scaled that barrier using her wit, her humor and a good-sized grappling hook called attraction. Now that he finally admitted to himself that he was growing serious about her, about them, she was backing away.

Why?

It was as if she had felt safe being herself as long as there was no danger that he would take her up on anything. It just didn't make any sense to him. She wasn't what guys in his younger years had called a tease.

And yet, that was what it seemed like to the outside observer.

He didn't want to be an outside observer. Not any longer.

With a sigh, Bruce went to join her. Maybe he could sort this out with her, clear up whatever misunderstanding was at the bottom of this before it became some sort of major obstacle between them. He didn't want obstacles between them.

As he tried to get to the buffet, he found his path blocked by Giovanni. The latter was obviously availing himself of the opportunity of finding him alone to talk.

He had no desire to talk to Giovanni, not when he was preoccupied with Margo. But it looked as if he had no choice.

Giovanni appeared to want to assure himself that there were no hard feelings. He clapped his hand on Bruce's shoulder, one comrade-in-arms in the battle between the sexes to another.

"You know, my friend, I admire a man who stands up for what is his."

His. It had a nice ring to it. But it was a false one.

He looked at the slighter man. It would have been easy, Bruce thought, to let Giovanni believe that he and Margo were a couple. That way he'd be making sure that there would be no trouble coming from the handsome Italian.

Easy, yes, but dishonest. And he had always been honest. Honest to a fault. It was too late to start something new at his age.

Was it? a small voice within him whispered. Was it really too late? Wasn't that the whole point of this? Of him and Margo? To start something new?

Point or not, letting Giovanni believe that they were a couple in every sense of the word wasn't right. It wasn't fair to Margo.

He'd deal with what was fair to himself later.

"If you're referring to Margo," he said quietly, "she's not mine."

Bruce looked around and saw her at the head of the buffet table, talking to the company's first VP. The man was laughing at something she'd just said. She had a talent for that, he thought, for making men feel good around her.

"No?" Giovanni looked surprised. Pleasure began to blossom in his face. "But the way you act, the way your eyes meet, I thought that…" He let his voice trail off significantly. When Bruce shook his head, Giovanni's smile widened. "Ah, then Margo is, how you say, fair play?"

"Game," Bruce corrected automatically. "Fair game. And she's not."

"But...oh, I see. You do want her. In this, you must see that you are not alone."

It wasn't a club competition, Bruce thought. But he had to concede at least that point to Giovanni. He realized he wasn't alone. As he looked at him, he could all but see the man rubbing his hands together.

"Well, until she makes up her mind, you will not fault me for dancing with her. She is a very desirable woman." He laughed softly to himself. When Bruce raised an inquiring brow at what he found so funny, Giovanni explained. "If she were mine, I would keep her under lock and key, for my eyes only." His smile was broad and downright wicked.

It was his own fault for being so honest, Bruce upbraided himself. But there wasn't anything he could do, other than to sternly point out, "We don't treat our women that way."

"Yes, I know." Giovanni nodded. "It is a pity for you, but very fortunate for me." He handed Bruce the glass of champagne he'd been sipping. "You will excuse me, I am suddenly feeling very hungry."

Bruce had no doubt that the hunger Giovanni was experiencing had very little to do with his stomach. He thought of going over to Margo himself. There was no doubt he'd get there first. He was the taller man, and his stride was definitely longer than Giovanni's.

But that would have been infantile, and one stern talk with himself was enough for the night. He wasn't about to descend into adolescent behavior again and take part in what amounted to a footrace.

Besides, he'd been right. No matter what he felt, no matter how he felt about her, he couldn't put restraints on Margo, even if she were his.

Which she wasn't.

Deciding to forgo the buffet, he went instead to the bar

to get himself a real drink. He set Giovanni's half-empty champagne glass on a side table as he strode past it.

"The evening went pretty well, don't you think?" Margo commented as they left the ballroom.

With his hand lightly against the small of her back, Bruce guided her toward the lobby. He was relieved to have her to himself again. Giovanni had all but monopolized Margo for the remainder of the evening.

"From Weston's standpoint," he agreed. "Marcello agreed to sign contracts in the morning."

She picked up on his tone. "And from your standpoint, how did the evening go?"

Bruce shrugged. He really didn't want to talk about it, but since she'd asked, "I got to see a side of myself I didn't like very much."

She knew what he was referring to. Another man might have caused a scene. He'd gallantly stepped aside, letting her make her own choices. You couldn't help but like a man like that. And she did. Maybe too much.

"You're being entirely too hard on yourself." They'd almost reached the revolving door when she remembered. Margo stopped, holding up her hand. "Wait, I almost forgot." She looked at him. "I need to stop by the front desk."

"Sure." He turned around and began to walk across the lobby again. "Why?"

"I have to leave Giovanni a message."

Her careless admission hit him with the force of an iron fist swung straight to the gut. Since they had just left the man less than three minutes ago, Bruce could only think that whatever message she had to leave for Giovanni was the kind of thing you didn't say aloud around other people.

He wasn't surprised, he supposed. Any woman would be flattered by Giovanni's attention, and he had certainly been attentive to Margo throughout the evening.

So much so that the flamboyant Italian representative had come perilously close to needing new dental work once or twice. Exercising extreme control had been the only way Bruce had managed to hold himself in check.

The desk clerk looked up as they approached. His genial smile went up a few more watts when he looked at Margo.

There was genuine enthusiasm in his voice as he asked, "Is there anything I can help you with?"

Margo opened her purse and took out a key. "Yes, would you give this to Mr. Giovanni Marcello?" She slid the key along the counter, pushing it toward the clerk. "He's in room 1209. Please tell him that the lady says thank you, but she won't be needing it."

With that, she threaded her arm through Bruce's and turned toward the front entrance again.

Walking beside her, Bruce could only stare at Margo, his power of speech all but gone. For a second he thought of wrapping his hands around Giovanni's aristocratically thin neck. The bastard had actually tried to arrange a tryst with Margo right under his nose.

"He gave you the key to his hotel room?" he finally asked.

Bruce's even voice wasn't fooling her. She'd seen enough covered boiling pots to know he was very close to blowing.

"That," she said offhandedly, as if it were a trinket housed in a box of cereal instead of an invitation to a night of seduction, "and a line that was very, very smooth."

He could feel the anger, the indignation at Giovanni's insult, draining slowly away. She was here with him, not riding the elevator to Giovanni's room. There was no reason to feel jealous. She'd made her choice. "But you didn't buy it."

She would have thought that was obvious. Her mouth curved. "Nope."

Letting Margo go out the door first, he was right behind her. "What was it?"

Margo turned and touched his cheek. "You don't want to hear."

No, he guessed he didn't. It was enough to hear that she had turned it down. He didn't want a reason to get angry. Anger clouded too many things.

Bruce handed his ticket to the valet, who went hurrying off to retrieve his car.

"Would you like to go somewhere?" he asked suddenly. By the look on her face, he knew he'd caught her completely off guard. "Dancing?" It was the first thing that came to mind.

She looked bemused. And just a touch bewildered. "I thought that's why we left, because you were tired of dancing."

"No," he contradicted, "I was tired of watching Giovanni dancing with you. And I was tired of Giovanni cutting in on us while we were dancing." Bruce slipped his arm around her shoulders, not possessively or to mark what was his, but because it felt right. "I'd like to hold you in my arms for a while and dance with you without feeling that annoying tap on my shoulder." He peered at her face. "Unless you're tired."

If she was, the feeling had completely vanished. She threw back her head, one earring brushing against her shoulder as she laughed. "Darling, I could dance until dawn."

He believed it.

Professionally, Bruce had to admit, things were falling into place very rapidly. Once Giovanni had signed the contracts for the merger of their two companies overseas the morning after the party in his honor, the date for opening the Florence office was moved up.

Bruce was told he had less than two weeks to get everything in order on the home front before he took the flight to Italy.

It didn't seem like nearly enough time.

All he actually needed, he told himself, was one evening. The right evening with the right setting.

And the right answer.

Determined, like a man with a mission, Bruce set things in motion. He made phone calls, went shopping and crossed his fingers.

There was a lot riding on this. It had been a long time since he had taken a personal risk. It occurred to him that he was getting back into the game with a doozy of a big one.

Johnny Mathis was softly crooning theme songs from old romantic movies on the CD player in Bruce's car as he drove.

He'd bought the CD just for her, Margo thought. She couldn't picture Bruce owning a CD like this of his own volition and yet he did.

He really was one in a million, she mused.

Turning toward him now, she looked at his profile. It was bathed half in shadow, half in moonlight. He appeared so rugged, so strong, it was hard to imagine the gentler, kinder emotions that dwelled just beneath the surface.

"You're being incredibly mysterious about this," she commented.

Bruce merely glanced in her direction without commenting, adding to the mystery.

They were driving down the Pacific Coast Highway. On her right, the ocean shimmered, warm and inviting, beneath the moonlight. The moon was full and cast a long, pale yellow line that skipped along the waters, leading off into eternity.

She hadn't a clue what was going on.

Bruce had called her at Melanie's shop just before closing time and asked to see her tonight. She'd agreed without a moment's hesitation. He was leaving at the end of the week. Five days from now, except for the occasional holiday and family get-together when they both found themselves on the same side of the same continent, he would be out of her life.

The thought brought a pang to her heart and filled her with an urgency she was unaccustomed to. An urgency to get in as much time with him as she possibly could. Before it was over.

"Over" the way all things were eventually over, she reminded herself.

She was glad he'd called. If he hadn't, she would have called him. She didn't believe in standing on ceremony or adhering to the rules of any game still being played between the sexes. It would have been a shame to waste these last few days by being apart.

"Shouldn't you be home, packing?" she asked when he still said nothing. He was being awfully quiet tonight. "I can help," she offered with growing enthusiasm. "I'm very good at packing. I've been living out of a suitcase for more than the last three years now, so that makes me an expert."

Packing was the last thing on his mind. He hoped none of his instructions had been overlooked. "I've got time to pack."

Margo could only shake her head. "Typical male thinking." Although it was probably the only thing about him that was typical, she added silently. "You leave it all to the last minute, then throw things haphazardly into a suitcase, rushing to catch your plane. You arrive at your destination with wrinkled clothes that you don't even need and find that you have to run out to buy underwear and socks, because you forgot to pack any."

He laughed at her scenario. All too true, probably, although he had managed fairly well on his previous business trips.

But this wasn't a trip, he reminded himself, this was a prolonged stay.

"All right," he allowed magnanimously, "when the time comes, I'll let you help."

"Let me?" she echoed mockingly. Despite the fact that she was restrained by the seat belt, she turned completely around to face him, feigning umbrage. "I'll have you know it's a privilege watching me pack."

"Then I'll be looking forward to it," he said with more feeling than she thought the situation warranted.

Margo sat back and studied him. Just what did he mean by that?

Chapter Twelve

He wouldn't answer her questions no matter how subtly she prodded.

Margo was torn between feeling amused, feeling frustrated and feeling just the slightest bit agitated.

She didn't like not knowing. If you didn't know, you weren't prepared, and she firmly believed, despite her blasé attitude, in being prepared.

For everything.

But no matter how she tried to worm the information out of him, Bruce merely gave her an enigmatic smile and said that she would find out where they were going soon enough.

She sighed and sat back. And waited. Bruce apparently wasn't a man to be budged once he made up his mind. Any other time, she might have admired his strength of character, but not when it was pitted against her.

The Pacific Coast Highway gracefully sashayed its way through the art community that had settled in along the picturesque shores of Laguna Beach. The colony had left small shops, museums and trendy restaurants in its wake to mark its progression. It was still just as charming as she remembered it.

It was like coming home, she realized with an unexpected tug at her heart. Her memory shuffled through the picture postcards in her mind, recalling happy days, days she'd spent with Melanie when both of them were growing up.

"I haven't been here in years," she confided. Pleasure filled her voice as she looked around. It seemed almost magical in the moonlight. Or was that because he was here beside her? "I always loved coming here."

Margo leaned forward, trying to make things out in the artificial glow of streetlights. The scenic arrangement of living quarters and hotels approximated a Mediterranean coastline, allowing her to visually enjoy the best of both worlds.

He glanced at her as he searched for the street he wanted. They were all so tiny, it was easy to miss in the semidarkness.

She was positively glowing. He'd made the right decision. "Yes, I know."

His words pulled her back. "How?"

Still looking for the turnoff, he didn't see the wary look entering her eyes. "Melanie told me."

Margo didn't understand. "Why would Melanie do that?"

"It just came up in the conversation," he said vaguely.

He didn't bother adding that the conversation had centered on finding the right setting in which he would propose to her. Bruce knew just how important proper settings were to Margo, and he figured he needed all the help he could get.

He saw she wasn't quite satisfied. "Favorite spots in California, things like that. Melanie said that you and she used to come here all the time when she was a little girl."

Placated, Margo relaxed again and nodded. "We'd come

early, while it was still overcast. That way we had the beach to ourselves for a while. Elaine never cared for the sand, so it was just Melanie and me—and a vat of suntan lotion made three.'' She treasured that time. She always would. ''We stayed all day,'' she added when he looked at her. ''That necessitates a lot of suntan lotion unless we wanted to look like lobsters.'' She glanced down at her fair skin. It seemed even paler in the moonlight. ''Are we going to a restaurant here?'' She wondered if they had all changed by now.

''In a manner of speaking.'' It was a restaurant that had agreed to cater the meal for him. A French restaurant that he knew without being told Margo would love.

Love being the active word here, he mused.

He was being deliberately difficult. ''Picnic on the beach?'' she guessed again.

There it was, Bruce thought, spotting the restaurant. Right where it was supposed to be, at the next light. He glanced at her as he slowed down for the turn. ''You really hate not knowing things, don't you?''

She pretended to eke the answer out between gritted teeth. ''With a passion.''

He laughed, making the right turn. ''Your ordeal is almost over.''

Bruce turned down a street that looked out directly onto the beach below. Again, it was like the merging of two different worlds. The area between the beach and the pavement was a hilly terrain covered with hearty grass, vegetation where entire generations of squirrels lived, and an ancient, gnarled tree. The latter had long ago laid down a section of its bark, allowing it to creep along the grass as it grew. Now it resembled a giant, stretched out on the grass, propping up his shaggy head as he rested.

For Margo the feeling of charged excitement, of homecoming grew. The years melted away. It was as if she'd never left.

"I remember this." Margo sat forward, on the edge of her seat. "There used to be a gazebo farther down." She pointed in the general direction. "Just before the path leading down to the beach."

"There still is." He kept his voice mild, slightly distracted, afraid she'd pick up on his intentions before he had a chance to surprise her with them. Parking at a meter that was halfway to the gazebo and his goal, Bruce got out and fed quarters into it as Margo exited the car on her side.

Rounding the trunk, she thought she could make out the edge of the gazebo's wooden roof. She stood on her toes to get a better view, but there were several trees in the way.

"You're right, it's still there."

She tugged on his arm, wanting to verify the gazebo's existence as quickly as possible. She felt like a child, returning to a beloved playground.

It was just as she remembered it, except that there was a newer roof on it. And someone had thought to put up a guardrail to keep people from leaning over too far. There was approximately a three-hundred-foot drop from the edge of the gazebo down to the beach below.

It took her a moment to see the table.

When she did, she stared at it, moving closer. There was a table in the middle of the gazebo. Covered with a lacy white tablecloth, with two tall, gray-blue candles in the center, it was set for two. A thick, velvet rope served as a boundary line, keeping her from gaining entry.

"Oh." Disappointment coupled with wistfulness floated through her sigh. "I guess someone's having a private party here."

"Yes." Bruce removed the rope that the maître d' had placed there only ten minutes before. "We are."

"You did this?" Her eyes widened. How impossibly romantic, she thought. Margo tried not to let it undo her too much, but she was already too late.

The man was just getting better and better. She was really going to miss him.

Bruce glanced over his shoulder toward the restaurant that stood adjacent to the gazebo and saw the maître d' through the window. The man was watching them. Making eye contact, he smiled and nodded at Bruce, apparently satisfied that he had followed instructions to the letter.

Taking Margo's arm, Bruce ushered her into her seat. "Strictly speaking, Philippe did it, but I made the arrangements."

She looked at him as he sat down. "Philippe?"

"The maître d' from the restaurant." He nodded toward the building. But Philippe was no longer at the window, having apparently gone on to tend to his other duties.

"Well, both of you certainly know how to set a table and get to a woman's heart." Margo removed the cover from her dish and found lobster Newburg waiting to delight her palate.

She raised her eyes to his as a disquietude nudged at her. He was going to an awful lot of trouble to make this a memorable evening. "Melanie again?"

Streamers of pale moonlight sneaking in over his shoulder bathed Margo's skin, made her look almost ethereal. Bruce set his own cover on the side table Philippe had provided. "She's very helpful, your daughter."

"And very secretive." Just the slightest frown formed on her brow, then vanished again. "I worked with her all day, and she didn't say a word about this." You would have thought Melanie would have at least hinted something was going on instead of acting surprised when Bruce called.

Good girl, he thought. He knew he could count on Melanie. "I asked her not to."

So much for loyalty, Margo thought. "At the risk of sounding monotonous, why?"

He reached across the table, covering her hand with his.

It was all the contact he allowed himself right now. "Because then it would spoil the surprise."

"I see." She bit back the urge to ask what surprise, knowing she was beginning to sound like Johnny One-Note. But Margo sincerely hoped that he was only referring to the dinner itself and not something more.

Something that would ruin everything.

Bruce saw the tiny furrow form between her brows. It wasn't quite the reaction he had hoped for, he thought. But maybe he was reading too much into it.

Taking the bottle of wine that Philippe had left chilling for them, Bruce filled her glass, then his own. His eyes on hers, he lifted the glass in a toast. "To the future."

They'd had this toast before, she thought. It was her toast. Then it had merely been a nebulous phrase, now it referred to a future that would see them going off in different directions. She didn't know if she was all that crazy about the future right now, even though she knew, at bottom, that what was going to happen was necessary. What was going on now in the present, this magical interlude, couldn't be expected to continue.

The worst thing in the world would be if she let herself believe that it could. Because if she believed, she'd be at risk of being beaten down again. There was no way she was going to take that kind of risk. She'd risk anything else but that. She couldn't live through it again and survive.

Margo substituted a more pleasing toast. "Let's drink to the moment instead."

"All right." He touched the rim of his glass to hers. A tiny "clink" resulted. "To the moment."

As she took a sip of wine, letting it slowly slide down her throat, Bruce felt his gut tighten. Maybe the toast was prophetic. Maybe he should seize the moment, not waiting until after dinner.

He wasn't sure he could, anyway.

Setting his glass down, he reached into his pocket for

the ring that was housed there. The ring he'd been carrying around all day like a talisman.

Fear leaped into her eyes as she saw him reaching into his jacket. An instinct for self-preservation had her quickly grabbing his wrist.

"What are you doing?"

He had no idea why she looked so frightened. He dropped his hand from his pocket. This needed a preamble, anyway. Not that he had one.

Bruce felt his way around. This wasn't as easy as he'd thought, but then, putting yourself on the line never was. "I'm afraid I don't have a gift for making flowery speeches like Giovanni."

There was no comparison between the two men. "You have attributes of your own," she said with a smile, trying to calm down. "And what you say is sincere, which means a lot to a woman, trust me. Giovanni, well, he's like a very sexy prerecorded message. Well rehearsed, but with no substance."

He liked that description. "I'm glad you feel that way, because then you won't mind if I stumble and trip over my own tongue." His smile was rueful as he looked at her. "I've been doing that a lot since you came along."

Bruce took a deep breath, bracing himself. It occurred to him that he felt less intimidated by the prospect of facing a root canal than what he was about to say, but then, there was a great deal more riding on this.

"I don't know any other way to say this, but to say it." He took her hand in his. "I never thought I'd love anyone else besides Ellen, but I was wrong. I love you, Margo."

She could feel her heart swelling, pulling toward him even as panic engulfed her. She hadn't wanted it to come to this, to declarations of feelings. Because what she was feeling most acutely was afraid. She was afraid, violently afraid, of loving him.

Of what loving him would mean to her.

She pulled back her hand, looking away. Looking everywhere but at his face. "I—I don't really know what to say."

Hurt scratched at him with tiny, sharp claws but he ignored it. This wasn't the time to lick wounds.

"Usually something like, 'I love you, too,' works well right about here." He looked into her eyes, searching for a sign that she reciprocated his feelings. He thought she had, but now he wasn't sure. "Florence would be a wonderful place for a honeymoon."

Margo pressed her lips together. Nerves jangled, threatening to unravel. "I'm sure a lot of people think so." Avoiding his eyes, she picked up her glass. Her hand was trembling so hard, she spilled a little of the wine on the tablecloth. Tiny amber pools mingled with the lace, staining it. She clutched at the diversion. "Damn, now you'll probably have to pay Philippe extra."

"The hell with the tablecloth." He took the glass from her hand. Her skin felt like ice. Why? It wasn't cold out. What was wrong? "Margo, in case I'm making such a mess of it that you're missing the point, I'm asking you to marry me."

She felt cornered, trapped, with nowhere to run. But there had to be. There'd always been somewhere to run before.

"I know what you're doing, Bruce, and I don't want you to do it, because then I'll have to say no and hurt you, and I don't want to hurt you." She blinked, feeling tears gathering. Damn him, anyway. "I don't want to hurt anyone. I just—oh, why did you have to do this?"

Margo felt as if she were being torn in two. If life had been different, if she still believed in those happy Hollywood endings that her aunt and her daughter believed in, she would have said yes. Shouted yes.

But she didn't believe, because she knew better. Knew

firsthand that men didn't stick around, that they disappointed you.

Feeling lost, desperate for a way out, Margo bolted from the table.

"Margo, wait," he called after her as she ran down the path to the beach. "Where are you going?"

She didn't answer. Because she didn't know. All she knew was that she had to get away from him. Before she made a fatal mistake, and said yes, the way something was desperately pleading with her to.

She ran blindly, unable to see because of the tears in her eyes, the tears that were flowing down her cheeks. Sand filled her shoes, pulling at them, slowing her down.

Stunned, Bruce called after her again, but she just kept running. For a moment he thought of letting her go. If she didn't want him, he wasn't going to push, wasn't going to demand a reason why she was throwing happiness, both his and hers, away. He wasn't going to—

The hell he wasn't.

He took off after her.

A marriage proposal wasn't supposed to bring tears of anguish to someone's eyes, Bruce knew. There was something else going on here, something he didn't understand, but he damn well intended to.

He caught up to her halfway down the beach. He grabbed her by the arm and swung her around to face him. "You move damn quick for a woman in high heels," he commented, trying hard to control the anger that fought for control of him. Being angry wasn't going to solve anything.

She gulped in air, trying to steady her racing pulse. "Practice."

He didn't smile. "Why, how many proposals have you run from?"

Margo took a deep breath, but she couldn't stop the trembling inside. "Yours is the first."

He shook his head, that wouldn't wash anymore. "I can't believe that no one's ever asked you to marry him before."

"Believe it." A rueful smile played on her lips. "I never stuck around long enough for it to go that far. I was usually gone as soon as the first sign cropped up that anything serious was going to happen."

Why? What was she so afraid of? "You didn't this time."

No, she didn't. She'd hung around, physically and emotionally hungry for more, just a little more. That had been her mistake. Greed. And now she was paying the price. The price of changing a beautiful memory into a sad one. Why couldn't he just leave well enough alone?

She shrugged, looking away. "I'm getting slower in my old age."

He brushed his hand along her cheek. Margo struggled not to lean into it.

Bruce saw the muted desire in her eyes. "You're not old, Margo. But I want to be there with you when you are."

She wasn't going to listen, wasn't going to let herself fall for a dream. "No, you don't. Those are just words. Nothing but words."

He was beginning to understand. "Yes, they are, but they're my words, Margo. My words and my honor. When have I lied to you?"

There was a lump growing in her throat. A lump that threatened to choke her. "I don't know."

"I haven't," he snapped, then caught himself. When she began to turn away, he placed his hands on her shoulders, holding her in place, forcing her to look at him. "Damn it, Margo, don't you think I don't know what's going on in your head?"

She raised her chin. Her voice was shaky. "If you did, you wouldn't have proposed."

"I said I know what's going on in your head," he said gently. "I also know what's going on in your heart." A defensive expression came over her face, but it faded as she looked up at him. "The same thing that's going on in mine. I love you, Margo, and I don't want you leaving my life. Ever."

She wasn't going to believe him, she wasn't. She couldn't. She knew what would happen if she did. "That's what you say now, but—"

"Ever," he repeated more forcefully. "There is no 'but,' Margo. With all due respect to Thomas Jefferson, all men are *not* created equal. I'm not your father and I'm not Melanie's father, or any other man who was stupid enough and insensitive enough to disappoint you in some way. I have no intention of disappearing out of your life." He held her fast, having nothing to work with but what was in his heart. He had to get through to her. "It's taken me a long time to open my heart again, but I have, and now you're in it. I'm not about to let you out." He dropped his hands to his side. It was the look in his eyes holding her in place now. "I'm here to stay, and you'd better get used to it."

No he wasn't. "You're leaving for Florence," she reminded him.

He meant what he said. "Not without you."

"And if I don't come?"

He didn't even hesitate for a heartbeat. "Then I don't go."

He looked as if he meant it, but it could all be just a bluff. Jack had sworn undying love just to get her to bed with him. "I had a job offer from DataLinc to go to France."

The news felt like a sharp knife in his heart. "Turn it down."

"And if I won't?" She watched his face, his eyes, waiting for a glimmer of betrayal. "If I want to go to France?"

If that was what she wanted, then that was what he wanted. "Then I'll go to France with you."

"And do what?" Margo challenged. Behind her, the surf

roared, pounding the shore with foamy capped waves as a seagull screeched, calling to its mate. There was a storm coming, she thought.

There was a storm already here.

The answer came easily. "Make love with you by night. I figure that'll more than compensate for anything I have to do by day to get by."

She felt herself yearning to believe him, struggling not to. "You'd do that? Leave a company you've been with for years? For me?"

One by one, he knocked down the obstacles. "Yes, yes and yes. Anything else?"

She looked into his eyes and saw that he meant it. Really meant it. He was willing to make sacrifices for her and all he asked in return was that she marry him. It probably didn't seem like such a huge sacrifice from where he was standing.

From where she was standing, it felt like it was a sheer drop.

But the beach was slowly getting closer.

Margo twisted her fingers together. "You know, I don't want to love you." She saw his eyes light up as hope entered them. "Tried very hard not to love you. But I don't seem to have a choice in the matter." She pressed her lips together as a sob threatened to come out. "That's what's so scary. I don't have a choice."

He reached for her. She didn't have to make any confessions to him, not when they were so painfully difficult to her. He didn't need her baring her soul, he just needed her to love him.

"Margo—"

She moved out of reach. If he touched her, she knew she'd cry and she wanted to get this out. He needed to know.

"Let me finish. Just before Melanie was born, I wrote to Jack, to let him know where I was. Part of me still thought that he would realize how much he really loved me and would come looking for me. The letter was sent back, marked 'Return to Sender.' It was in his handwriting. He hadn't even bothered to open it. I was carrying his child and he didn't even want to know if I was all right, if I needed anything. If the baby needed anything.''

There was a hot, dry feeling in her throat. She'd cried out her tears over Jack a long time ago.

He listened, hating the man who had done this to her, who'd destroyed the young, loving girl she'd been. He vowed he would make it up to her.

''I swore to myself that I was never going to be in that position again. I was never going to let a man be in charge of my heart.'' She turned around, raising her eyes to his. ''If—if I give it to you—''

He'd held himself in check long enough. Bruce took her into his arms. ''I swear I'll take good care of it.''

She took a deep breath. God, but it did feel good, having him hold her. Keeping the world at bay. She let herself absorb the feeling, savoring it.

She raised her head, looking at him. ''I can give you an answer to your proposal in seven languages, you know. Eight if you count the one I'm just learning.'' She was scared. Scared to say yes, but far more scared to say no and lose him. ''Which would you like to hear?''

The wind was toying with her hair, playing with the ends. He smoothed them back. ''I don't care, as long as the answer's yes. Is it?''

She threw her arms around his neck, embracing him, embracing love. *''Si.''*

He grinned. ''Italian, right?''

Margo laughed. ''You're going to go far.''

''Lady, you have no idea,'' he promised her just before he kissed her.

Epilogue

Lance made no effort to hide his amusement as he watched his father re-tie his tie for the seventh time. "Were you this nervous when you married Mom?"

Bruce shifted, glaring into the mirror within the small room. He could do this in his sleep, why couldn't he tie this damn thing today of all days. Letting the ends drop, he tried again.

"I don't know. It was so long ago. Probably," he mumbled, preoccupied. He was straining to listen for some sound that would tell him Margo had finally arrived at the church and wasn't checking in at the local airport. "No, wait, I knew where your mother was fifteen minutes before the ceremony started. She was in the church, getting ready." He yanked the ends in frustration. The tie drooped. "I have no idea where Margo is, or even if..."

Standing behind his father, Lance took over. Two smooth movements later, the tie was in place. "She'll be here."

Bruce turned around to face his son. "I'd feel a whole lot better if that was her saying that."

Lance paused, replaying the comment in his head.

"There'd be no need for her to assure you of her coming if she were here, saying it."

"Exactly." The slight knock on the door had his wide shoulders stiffening. He swung around, only to see Bess peering in. "Any sign of her?"

Bess gave him a heartening smile. "Don't worry, Bruce. She'll be here."

Margo's face floated through his mind. Not when she finally agreed to his proposal, but before. When fears and insecurities had threatened to tear down what was being built up between them. He was a realist. "What if she's not?"

Unfazed, Bess, who was standing in the room, shifted her glance toward her nephew. "Then we'll just have to hunt her down and shoot her, won't we, Lance?"

Lance grinned. "I think Melanie might have something to say about that." A large bang suddenly echoed through the chamber. The front doors of the church had been thrown open and then fell shut again. Lance looked at his father. "Hear that? That's the sound of a woman rushing to her own wedding."

Bruce's mouth curved. Thank God. "Better late than never."

Bess patted his arm. Her brother was one in a million. "That woman's got herself a great catch in you."

Melanie rolled her eyes as she helped her mother hurry into the long white gown. The brocade skirt fell arrow straight to the floor. "You certainly like to cut things down to the wire, don't you?"

"It wasn't a wire, it was a garter." Margo could almost feel it hugging her thigh. She was almost surprised she could push the words out. Her throat felt so tight.

Melanie stopped fussing with the skirt. "What?"

"I was almost here when I remembered that I was supposed to have something old." Margo's eyes met Melanie's in the mirror. "You know, something borrowed, something blue, something old, something new. I doubled back to get this." Raising the skirt, she showed off the slightly faded, delicate blue and white garter. "Marlene Dietrich wore this in *Destry Rides Again.* Aunt Elaine always teased me and said she wanted to give me that to wear if I ever finally walked down the aisle."

As Melanie slipped the veil into place on her hair, Margo stared in the mirror as if she'd never seen the woman looking back at her. Her face was flushed with excitement. "You don't think this is too much, do you? The dress I mean."

"The dress isn't too much." Standing behind her mother, Melanie slipped her arms around her waist and gave her a quick, heartfelt squeeze. She was so happy for her mother, she could cry. "It's beautiful, just like you are, Mama. Every bride deserves to look gorgeous on her wedding day."

"Wedding day," Margo echoed. It seemed incredible. "I was sure this day would never come for me."

Melanie glanced at her watch. Show time. "That's not all that'll be coming for you if you don't hurry out of this room. 'The Wedding March' is starting."

Margo pressed her fingers to her stomach, willing the fluttering to stop. It didn't.

When she didn't move, Melanie very gently hooked her arm through her mother's and drew her out of the room. "We can't fit all the people in here, Mama. You're going to have to go out to them."

But for Margo, there was no "them," there was only Bruce.

All through the long walk down the aisle, she kept her eyes trained on the man at the front of the church, the man who had come to rescue her heart from a cold legacy. The man she was going to spend the rest of her life with.

She looked like a vision, floating toward him. Bruce

could hardly believe that she was really here now, beside him. ''What took you so long?'' he whispered as she laid her hand on his arm.

Together, they turned toward the priest. ''I have no idea,'' she replied. ''But I'm here now.''

He felt himself relaxing as happiness pushed aside the tension. ''That's all that counts,'' Bruce told her.

And it was.

$$* \quad * \quad * \quad * \quad *$$

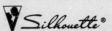

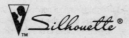

Based on the bestselling miniseries

FORTUNE'S *Children*™

A FORTUNE'S CHILDREN *Wedding:*
THE HOODWINKED BRIDE

by BARBARA BOSWELL

This March, the Fortune family discovers a twenty-six-year-old secret—beautiful Angelica Carroll *Fortune!* Kate Fortune hires Flynt Corrigan to protect the newest Fortune, and this jaded investigator soon finds this his most tantalizing—and tormenting—assignment to date....

Barbara Boswell's single title is just one of the captivating romances in Silhouette's exciting new miniseries, **Fortune's Children: The Brides,** featuring six special women who perpetuate a family legacy that is greater than mere riches!

Look for *The Honor Bound Groom,* by Jennifer Greene, when **Fortune's Children: The Brides** launches in Silhouette Desire in January 1999!

Available at your favorite retail outlet.

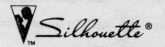

Silhouette®

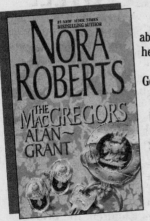
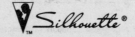

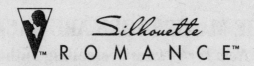

™ R O M A N C E™

COMING NEXT MONTH

#1354 HUSBAND FROM 9 TO 5—Susan Meier
Loving the Boss

For days, Molly Doyle had thought she was Mrs. Jack Cavanaugh, and Jack played along—then she got her memory back, and realized she was only his *secretary*. So how could she convince her bachelor boss to make their pretend marriage real?

#1355 CALLAGHAN'S BRIDE—Diana Palmer
Virgin Brides Anniversary/Long Tall Texans

Callaghan Hart exasperated temporary ranch cook Tess Brady by refusing to admit that the attraction they shared was more than just passion. Could Tess make Callaghan see she was his truelove bride before her time on the Hart Ranch ran out?

#1356 A RING FOR CINDERELLA—Judy Christenberry
The Lucky Charm Sisters

The last thing Susan Greenwood expected when she went into her family's diner was a marriage proposal! But cowboy Zack Lowery was in desperate need of a fiancée to fulfill his grandfather's dying wish. Still, she was astonished at the power of pretense when *acting* in love started to feel a lot like *being* in love!

#1357 TEXAS BRIDE—Kate Thomas

Charming lawyer Josh Walker had always wanted a child. So when the woman who saved him from a car wreck went into labor, he was eager to care for her and her son. Yet lazy days—and nights—together soon had Josh wanting to make Dani *his*…forever!

#1358 SOLDIER AND THE SOCIETY GIRL—Vivian Leiber
He's My Hero

Refined protocol specialist Chessy Banks Bailey had thirty days to transform rough 'n' rugged, true-grit soldier Derek McKenna into a polished spokesman. Her mission seemed quite impossible…until lessons in etiquette suddenly turned into lessons in love.…

#1359 SHERIFF TAKES A BRIDE—Gayle Kaye
Family Matters

Hallie Cates didn't pay much attention to the new sheriff in town—until Cam Osborne arrested her grandmother for moonshining! Hallie swore to prove her grandmother's innocence. But she was soon caught up in the strong, passionate arms of the law herself!